The Unknown Truth

Annette Labelle

A copy of this book has been lodged with the British
Library in London, England.
Copyhouse Press Ltd
International House, 24 Holborn Viaduct
London
United Kingdom, EC1A 2BN

ISBN 9780993394027

Dedication

This book would not have been possible without the help of my husband, James Labelle. You sat by me and helped me with ideas every time you saw me struggling. If not for you, this book would not be finished. Thank you and I love you.

To my sister, Christina Pereira, thank you for listening patiently to my rambling on and on about The Unknown Truth. Your encouraging words helped me to keep going and finish this book.

To my parents, Ronald and Jeannette Walker, thank you for making me believe that I can do anything. You've always stuck by me and made me realize that anything is possible. I can only hope that I make my children feel as special as you make me.

To my children, Janice, Alexus and Hudson, thank you for patiently waiting for mommy to get off of the computer to play with you. I love the three of you so much.

To my brother, Danny Walker, just read it… you know you want to!

Acknowledgements

To Lauren Lalonde, for your patience, understanding and being a fantastic editor. I'd still be looking for my grammar mistakes if it weren't for you.

To Suzanne Hyland, thank you for inspiring me to continue to write this book when I felt like I had hit a wall. Your stories and encouragement helped bring this book to where it is today.

To everyone's real life ghost stories that inspired me to make this book a little creepier, thank you.

To everyone who proofread my book and gave me feedback on it, thank you.

Finally, to everyone who reads my book, thank you for giving me a chance and I hope you enjoy it!

The Unknown Truth

Prologue

The trees surrounded me but I managed to run by each one without stopping or hitting any of them. I looked back and I didn't see him anymore. *I've outrun him*, I thought. I stopped for a second to breathe and to take in my surroundings but, before I could do that, I heard a branch snap and the sound of dry leaves crumbling. I looked back and there he was running full force towards me. I exhaled and ran. I ran with every ounce of energy I could find, when suddenly I fell. I tripped over a root that stuck up from the ground and I landed face first into the muddy path. I tried to stand but my legs wouldn't work. I tried to scream but nothing came out. I looked behind me and there he was. He stood above me, just for a second, before he reached down to grab me.

Chapter 1

My eyes snapped open to the sound of a knock on my bedroom door. I tried to ignore it. *Boom, boom, boom,* the sound of the fist against my door rang through my ears. I covered my head with my pillow. *Go away,* I thought to myself, but I wouldn't actually say that out loud. I knew it was my mother on the other side of the door. I could hear her sighs of annoyance. She really despised the thought of my idea of getting a lock on my door.

"I'm seventeen, Mom. I need my privacy!" I remember shouting when she objected.

I didn't dislike my mother, we actually got along really well, and we still do. But like any other teenager, I sometimes had an attitude.

"Tina, you need to get up and get ready for school!" I heard my mother speak through the cracks of my door.

I knew she wouldn't stand at my door for too long as she had to tend to my two year old sister and nine month old brother.

"You're going to be late!" she said sternly but I didn't reply. I waited silently for a few more moments to see when she would give up.

Finally, I thought to myself when I heard her footsteps fade down the stairs.

I closed my eyes for a few more minutes before I stretched all the sleep out of my body. I sat up and looked around my room. We had moved into this house about two weeks ago. I liked my new room; it was big, it was cozy and I had a lock on my door. I smiled to myself. There was no real reason why I wanted the lock on my door. Maybe it was because my best friend Emily had one or maybe it was because I wanted to see what my parents would say. I hopped out of bed and went to my closet. I pulled out a pair of jeans and a blue t-shirt. I laid my clothes on my bed then unlocked and opened my door.

"I'm up Mom," I shouted down the stairs. "I'm going to take a shower."

We all shared one bathroom in our house. I didn't mind. I was the only one that used it really. My mother and father just went in to do their business, so the washroom was usually available. My sister and brother were too young to use it and by the time they'd need it I might be living on my own.

I took a hot, steaming shower and let the water soak me for a little while. After my shower, I towel dried myself and put on my robe. My room was the closest to the washroom, so I opened the door and ran to it. I hated being cold. I closed and locked my door, took off my robe and slipped back under my covers until I was completely dry and warm. I looked over at my clock, "Shoot!" I threw the blankets off of me and got dressed as quickly as

I could. I stood in front of my long mirror and looked at myself. I was about 5 feet 6 inches tall, slim but I hid my figure behind my baggy clothing. I was never comfortable wearing form fitting clothes. I never liked attention, so the more I blended into my clothes, the better. My hair was blonde and long; it went down to the middle of my back. It was straight and there was no wave to it so I wore it down most of the time. Today, though, it was going in a ponytail because I had no time to blow dry it. I had blue eyes that I highlighted with black eyeliner and that was the extent of my makeup routine in the mornings.

I ran down the stairs and into the kitchen. My mother was feeding my little brother, Tommy.

"Well, well, Miss Tina Trudent, good morning," my mother said to me with annoyance still dripping off of her words.

"Good morning, Mom!" I smiled at her. "I love you," I said through my smile. She couldn't help but smile back and tell me that she loved me too.

"Hey, Heidi, good morning to you," I said to my little sister who was two hands deep in her milky cereal. I laughed at her as I pulled her hands out and wiped them on a cloth.

"Morning, Tina," she replied in her cute two year old voice.

I took a bowl out of the cupboard and poured myself some cereal and sat beside Heidi.

"We need you to watch the children on Saturday night. Can you do that for us?" my mother asked.

"Yes, but I have a school dance on Friday, remember? I can still go right?" I asked.

"Of course you can, Tina. Just remember your curfew is at eleven. Your Dad and I have a wedding to go to on Saturday, we won't be too late though," my mother explained.

"No problem, Mom," I said.

I drank my orange juice and excused myself from the table to get ready to leave for school. I gathered up my jacket and book bag and left for the day.

*****

Emily was my best friend. She was beautiful. She was just a little shorter than I was, maybe 5 feet and 3 inches tall, with dark brown, long curly hair. Her eyes matched her hair colour. We always met at the corner a block away from school, and of course she was waiting for me.

"What took you so long?" she said as I approached her.

"Sorry, my bed was very comfortable this morning," I smirked.

We walked the rest of the way to school and met up with some friends at the front doors. There was one guy in our group of friends that I was happy to see every morning.

11

"Hey Jack," I said shyly as he made eye contact with me. I hated when he did that. He would gaze at me with his brilliant blue eyes and he would wait for me to notice. It always caught me off guard and the butterflies went crazy in the pit of my stomach.

"Hey," he said as he hid a smile. He obviously saw how he affected me.

Jack was tall with reddish brown hair that went so well with his blue eyes. I shook my head and looked at Emily. That's all I had to do and she knew.

"Catch you guys later, we're heading in," she said for my benefit, which I was truly grateful for.

"Why don't you just ask him to the dance?" Emily said to me as we walked away. She added, "Everyone clearly sees the sparks between the two of you."

Really? I thought to myself, *he had sparks for me?* We headed to our lockers and then to our first period class. Emily and I had all but one class together. When I was in parenting class, she was in wood working class. She liked that class because she was the only girl. She was surrounded by boys for an hour and a half. I guess I can see why she liked it.

At break time, I went outside at the back of the school. That's where Jack went out for all of the school breaks. I waited for Emily before I walked over to him.

"Are you anxious for the dance?" Jack asked me as Emily and I approached him.

"Yes I am," I responded with a smile.

"Are you going with anyone?" he asked.

"No, just me and Emily," I said.

"Cool," he said and walked over to some guys we knew from class.

"What was that?" Emily asked as she elbowed me with a grin.

"I'm not sure," I said.

Emily and I took a walk around the whole outside of school to finish our break. Our school sat on an entire street block.

*****

After school, I went home and upstairs to my room. I thought about what Emily had said. Could I actually break down and ask Jack to go to the dance with me? Honestly, I couldn't do it. He was perfect in every way but if he didn't ask me, I would be going solo. We would meet up and hang out and that would be good too. I tried to convince myself, solely for the sake of not being rejected.

Eating supper in our new kitchen was different, but in a good way. We never had a kitchen that was so big. It was nice to have supper with everyone sitting around the table and talking about our day. Our old kitchen wasn't big enough to do that. I used to sit on the couch and watch TV as I ate my supper and my mother would put Tommy in his car seat, placing him on the floor beside her. Heidi sat in a highchair that took up most of the space in the kitchen and my father would sit at the head of the table.

"How was everyone's day?" my mother asked interrupting the silence.

"Mine was good. Everyone is excited about the dance on Friday!" I answered.

"That's nice, dear," she said.

We all sat, ate and talked about our day. After dinner, my mother gathered up all the dishes and put the condiments in the fridge. My job was the dishes. As I washed the dishes, I thought about what I was going to wear to the dance. It was only two days away. I was excited. I thought about wearing something completely different from my everyday style, which was anything that was not baggy and unflattering. *That would really turn heads*, I thought to myself. That's one thing I did not like to do. But, just that once, I didn't think it would be a problem, as long as one of the heads that I made turn was Jack's. I smiled and hummed as I finished drying the dishes. When I put the last dish away, I hurried out of the kitchen and went upstairs to my room to look at the clothes that I had to work with.

"Well, maybe if I took this dress and put these leggings under it, with this scarf..." I was talking to myself, as this was the sixth outfit I tried to put together.

Failing with every item of clothing that I chose, I gave up and went to my parent's room. I went straight to my mother's closet. It was a little chilly in their room, cooler than the rest of the house.

"What do you have for me to wear, Mom?" I was still talking to myself out of pure frustration.

I opened her closet door and found that there were so many dresses. I didn't know my mother owned such nice clothing. *We should fit in the same size clothes*, I observed. I closed my mother's closet door and ran downstairs to the living room.

"Mom, can I borrow one of your dresses for the dance?" I was out of breath, but a whole new feeling of excitement had overcome me. *It might not be hopeless after all*, I thought.

"Sure, just make sure it fits and not too much cleavage," she said. I thanked her and ran out of the room. "Not too short either, Tina!" she called as I ran up the stairs taking two steps at a time. I could hear the laughter in her voice as she gave me these rules. I couldn't blame her because I had never been interested in dressing up, let alone wearing a dress.

After trying on a few dresses, I decided on a blue one. It had thick straps and there were no rhinestones on it. It was plain with a pretty silver handbag hanging on the same hanger that the dress was on. I wore the dress well; no cleavage and it went down just below my knees. I was satisfied. *Shoes!* I thought, *oh no! I don't own pretty shoes!* But luckily, I looked down to the floor of the closet and there were some beautiful flat silver shoes.

"Perfect!" I said out loud and I tried them on.

They were a little tight but they would still work. I couldn't wipe the smile off my face, even if I tried.

"Mom!" I yelled down the stairs. "Can you come to your room? I found a dress but I want you to see it on me."

"Coming!" she yelled back up to me.

She came up to her room with Heidi on her hip. She sat Heidi on her bed and scanned me up and down. I was a little shy as this was not my sort of thing but she smiled in approval.

"It looks wonderful honey!" she said as she gave me a hug. "Do you want to borrow some earrings and maybe a nice necklace and bracelet?" she asked.

"Thanks Mom; let's see what you got," I replied with my eyes still locked on the image of myself in the mirror.

"Who are you going to this dance with?" my mother asked.

"Oh, just Emily, but we will meet up with others when we get there. I don't have a date, Mom," I laughed, because I knew that was the question that she really wanted to ask.

I walked away from my reflection in the mirror and went over to my mother's dresser, where she was already pulling out different pieces of jewelry. I looked over at Heidi, who was sitting very still and watching us. She was unusually quiet. Something about her made the hair on the back of my neck stand up. She was watching us with no interest, but her hair was moving. She seemed aware of the movement but didn't want to move. She didn't look scared; she just looked curious. The way her hair was moving looked as though some invisible hands were holding strands of her hair up in the air. But that was impossible. I continued to listen to my mother as she explained different ways to wear a certain necklace that she was holding up, but my eyes were glued on Heidi. I looked up to see if the ceiling fan was on, but it wasn't. I walked away from my mother, towards the window, with my eyes still on Heidi's moving hair. I parted the curtains. I knew very well that the window was closed because the curtains were still, but I checked anyway. It was closed. I was confused and I didn't want to scare Heidi so I walked over and picked her up. I acted as though nothing had happened and asked her if I looked pretty. Thankfully, her hair had stopped moving.

"You look like a princess, Tina," she squealed in delight.

"Well, thank you. You look as beautiful as a sparkly fairy!" I said as I covered her face in kisses.

My mother and I agreed on a small silver necklace and a pair of silver hoop earrings to match the hand bag and shoes. I didn't want to wear a bracelet.

"Thank you, Mom. Can I leave these in my room until Friday?" I asked.

"Sure," she answered.

I had a really hard time falling asleep that night. I couldn't think of any logical explanation for Heidi's hair. What was happening to it? Was it static electricity? I highly doubted that. I was mind boggled. I didn't tell my mother what I saw because I wasn't really sure what it was. I kept running the whole thing over in my head as I laid in my room and I wondered why I didn't tell my mother to just turn around. At least, then, we could try to figure this out together. My conclusion always ended the same way: I didn't want to scare Heidi.

*****

The next day at school, I asked Emily if she knew what she was wearing on Friday. She did, she always did. Emily was always very organized. She made me look and feel like a procrastinating fool. I told her all about the dress that my mother was going to let me wear and she told me what she was going to wear. She decided on a black skirt that went to her knees with a long black shirt, a purple belt and her black boots. I couldn't wait to see it all together. I couldn't wait to see if Jack noticed me.

It was yet another uneventful day at school. We went to all of our classes, took down notes and read out loud in our English class. We had book reports due that day. The book that we had to read was "The Outsiders." There were some kids who hadn't even started it. I had already read that book on my own time. I didn't tell anybody though. I was definitely a book worm, but nobody knew. All the book reports that were done, pretty much sounded the same. Some kids added fancy words to theirs but the overall result looked as though everyone had passed with the same grades.

*****

I opened my eyes on Friday morning and smiled to myself. *Finally*, I thought. It felt like this day would never come. I had been to plenty of school dances, but this was the first one that Jack would be attending. Knowing that Jack would be there made it very hard to hold in my excitement.

When I arrived at school, the hallways were buzzing. *Looks like I'm not the only one who is wound up*, I smiled as I thought of it. The whole school looked thrilled about that night's festivities. Girls were standing at their lockers comparing makeup and holding their hair up in different styles, asking for their friends' opinions. I hadn't thought about my hair, nor had I thought about my makeup but I wasn't concerned. I think that Jack seeing me in a dress will have a big enough impact. I didn't want to overdo it.

The school day unexpectedly flew by. I thought that it would be the longest day of the year.

Everyone was so hyped up about the dance, that school and homework were the last thing on everyone's minds. The teachers were very understanding and let the students get away with a lot of whispering during classes. At first break, Emily and I went outside to where Jack hung out and we waited. Jack never showed up.

"Is he not at school today?" I whispered to Emily.

"Now that I think about it, I haven't seen him this morning," she replied.

We gave up on waiting for Jack and did our usual walk around the perimeter of the school. When second break came around, we did the same thing and went out to the back of the school to look for Jack. He wasn't there. My heart sank in to the pit of my stomach. If he wasn't at school, he probably wouldn't be at the dance either.

The day went on and I gave up on seeing Jack at school, but I really hoped that I would see him that night.

*****

Emily came over and we got ready together. We did each other's hair, but we did our own makeup. Emily looked fantastic. She was so beautiful and the outfit really brought out that beauty. I was happy with my reflection. I looked so different. My hair and makeup were my usual style but you could actually see that I had a figure in the dress.

We hopped down the stairs to say goodbye to my parents. My father smiled and told us that we looked great, but my mother jumped out of her chair and went for the camera.

"Run, Emily!" I joked and we pretended to head for the door.

"Very funny," she said. "Now, stand together so I can get a nice one."

We did as she asked and smiled. After our picture, I gave both my parents a kiss on the cheek and we left.

We chose to walk. It was a nice night and we didn't want to arrive too early. As we walked, we laughed and talked. When the school came into view, it was surrounded by students from all four high schools in the city of Cornwall. I hadn't thought about that, so it instantly gave my stomach a twist and the butterflies went wild. Not that it mattered who would be there, I just wasn't expecting so many people. As we got closer to the school, my eyes instantly started scanning all the faces in search for Jack.

"I really hope he comes," I said to Emily. *Maybe he'll ask me to be his girlfriend*, I hoped.

We arrived at the front of the school and made our way through the crowd of students to the doors. There was a line up but it wasn't too bad; all the students were too busy socializing instead of getting in line. We met up with a few friends and we all stood in the short line. We all laughed and joked, but my eyes were still wandering and searching for one sweet face. We reached the front of the line and were given a bracelet to wear.

As we walked into the gymnasium, the wonderful decorations came into view. They did a great job of making the theme "Under the Sea" look like we were really under the sea. There were tropical fish ornaments hanging all over the place. The walls had drapes that looked like water. The whole gym was decorated perfectly. The speakers were blaring dance music and kids were dancing, jumping and laughing.

Emily and I went to dance with some friends. There was a screen up on the far wall that played the music video to each of the songs that we danced to. Everyone was dancing with their eyes glued to the screen; it was very cool. I was singing along to the music, dancing with my arms up high in the air and laughing with my friends. Every so often, I scanned the dance floor and the perimeter of the gym for Jack, but he was still nowhere to be found. I stopped dancing when the song ended and went to get a drink. Even the punch bowl had little toy fish floating around in it. I stood at the refreshment table, sipped my drink and picked at the snacks that were laid out.

Suddenly, there was a huge commotion by the doors that led outside. I stayed away. I didn't want to get involved, but I stayed where I was so I could have a good view as to what was happening. Finally, someone broke through the crowd of people, standing just away from everyone, and scrutinized the different groups of students until his eyes met mine. It was Pete, Jack's best friend. He ran over to me, grabbed my arm and started pulling me to the crowd of people blocking the doors. I fought him to let me go. He stopped and positioned himself in from of me, staring.

"Jack is outside and he wants to see you. They won't let him through the doors so he is causing a commotion out there," he explained.

I was so confused. Why won't they let him in? I followed Pete through the heavy crowd of people. I had to push my way through to keep up with him. The people that I pushed didn't even seem to notice that I was trying to get by. Finally, I broke through the incredibly large group and instantly wished that I hadn't. Jack was being held back by some of his friends, covered in blood, while he continuously called on this other guy to fight. From where I stood, it looked as though they had already fought and the other guy won, because he wasn't bleeding as much as Jack was. I looked around for Pete but he was already standing in front of Jack, yelling at him. Finally, Jack's attention was grabbed and he listened to what Pete was saying. Then, it hit me; those brilliant blue eyes with the sideways grin. Jack had spotted me and calmed down. *He was happy to see me?* I thought. Slowly and uneasily, his friends let him go and he walked over to me.

"Are you having fun?" Jack asked me in a very gentle voice.

23

I was too stunned to talk. I kept stealing glances at the other guy, who was still full of rage. "Who is that?" I asked. Jake looked back as though he had forgotten all about that guy.

"Oh, that guy? He is a jerk who beat the crap out of me and now, because of him, I can't go into the dance!" he shouted towards the other guy.

"Is he the reason that you weren't at school today?" I asked.

"Yes," he said.

"Well, what happened?" I asked so quietly. I wasn't sure that he had heard me.

"Don't worry about it, it's no big deal," he replied. I stared at him with my eyes as wide as quarters. *It's no big deal?* What a crazy thing to say!

"It had to be something bad. You're full of blood!" I commented.

He looked down at himself. "Yeah, that's why they wouldn't let me in the dance," he said, still shouting his words towards everyone else as he spoke to me.

All the bystanders were looking at us with concern, surprise, anger and laughter. I hated every second of it and I wanted to go back inside to get away from it all. I was embarrassed.

"Why did you want me to come outside?" I asked as I looked at the ground.

"I wanted to make sure that you were having fun. I wanted to be the one who asked you to dance and get you a drink. Is anyone doing that for you?" he asked.

"No, I was able to get my own drink, thanks." I was still looking down at the ground; I couldn't raise my eyes to meet his. "I'm going back in now. Emily is probably wondering where I am," I said as I started to walk away, still not making eye contact. "I will see you on Monday if you choose to come to school," I said without turning his way.

As I walked back toward the doors, Emily came racing out to see me.

"What's going on? Who is that guy? Why is Jack bleeding?" She had so many questions that I didn't have any answers for.

"Apparently, it's not a big deal and Jack has it all under control," I responded as I took Emily's arm and guided her back towards the school doors. At that moment, everyone got really loud behind me. I turned as my curiosity got the better of me, and I saw Jack walk over to the other guy and punch him in the face.

"That's what you get for ruining my chances with her!" Jack shouted at him. *Does he mean me?* I thought.

The other guy's friends let him go and it became a full blown fight between the two of them. He punched Jack in the face; his punch threw Jack back about five feet and onto his behind. Jack got back up. In the process of getting up, Jack kicked him directly across his knees, sending the other guy flying sideways and face first onto the cement. The fight continued and soon after the police showed up. Both guys were on the ground, making it easier for the police to make their arrests.

Emily and I pushed our way back through the crowd and went back to the gymnasium. The rest of the night didn't matter to me. I followed Emily around until she became annoyed and decided that it was time to leave. *Finally,* was all I could think to say, but I didn't say anything. I followed Emily out of the doors and she called her mother for a ride home. We waited at the side of the road in the front of the school until her mother arrived. We didn't really say much. I wasn't sulking, but I was disappointed. Emily's mother drove me home.

I was one hour early for my curfew so my mother was curious as to why I was home so early.

"There was a big fight outside school and it ruined a lot of moods, so most of us just went home," I explained. I was being vague; I didn't want to tell her much.

She accepted my justification and went back to her TV show. I went up to my room and took off my mother's dress and shoes and I put on my robe. I went to the washroom and drew a warm bubble bath. It felt so good to soak and forget about everything. I laid there for a while and decided that it was time to get out when my fingers looked like prunes. I reached over to unplug the drain when a horrific scream came from what sounded like downstairs. I froze in place and listened for any other commotions. I heard nothing, so I hurriedly unplugged my water and got out of the tub. I threw on my robe and opened the door. My mother was standing there with a look of fear, staring back at me.

"What happened?" I asked.

"I don't know, why did you scream?" she asked me.

"Mom, I didn't scream. The scream came from downstairs," I replied. She looked at me as though I were crazy.

"Tina, the scream came from the washroom, I was passing right by it when you screamed. I was on my way up to bed," she replied.

I stood there and stared at her. I didn't know what to say. The scream sounded like it came from downstairs. It wasn't clear enough to be from upstairs, let alone the room that I was in.

"Well, I didn't scream," I said as I dismissed the conversation and went to my room.

I closed and locked my bedroom door. I went over to my bed where my PJs were from that morning and I put them on. *What a night*, I thought, *this night couldn't get any worse*. I lay in my bed and forced my eyes shut and eventually fell asleep.

*****

"We won't be too late," my father said, grumbling as he put his jacket on over his shirt and tie that Saturday night.

My mother smiled towards him and agreed. They looked so young and beautiful. My father was very handsome in his black suit. My mother looked stunning in a beautiful dark purple dress with her hair in an up do. They were striking.

"Thank you, Tina," my mother said as she gave me a kiss on my forehead, and the two of them walked out the door.

"What do you rug rats wanna do?" I asked my sister and brother.

Heidi looked up at me with her bright blue eyes and said that she wanted to watch a movie. We pulled out all of the DVDs and spread them across the floor. Tommy crawled to them and slobbered all over the one that he picked up. I let him be as Heidi carefully chose the perfect movie for us to watch. After ten full minutes of deciding, she finally chose a cartoon princess movie.

"Do you want a snack?" I asked Heidi as she got comfortable.

I had just put Heidi in her one piece PJ. I was in the process of wrestling the slobber covered movie out of Tommy's hands as I put his PJs on him.

"Yes, I want pizza!" she yelled in a happy voice.

"Pizza! I don't think so little girl! How about some fishy crackers?" Of course, I won after I tickled the pout off of her cute little face.

"I love fishy crackers!" she exclaimed, knowing very well that she was defeated.

We all sat quietly and watched the princess movie. Tommy was fast asleep in my arms. Heidi had seen this movie a dozen times before, but she still sat quietly watching it with me. When the movie ended, I announced that it was bedtime. There were no complaints. I followed Heidi slowly up the stairs with Tommy still sleeping in my arms. We went into Tommy's room together and I slowly laid him in his crib. Heidi handed me a blanket that she wanted Tommy to sleep with and I tucked it all around him. When I was satisfied that he was comfortable, we went into Heidi's room to tuck her into her bed.

When we got to her room, she had a fit about wanting to sleep in mommy and daddy's bed. I knew that this wouldn't be a problem, because they could just pick her up and put her in her own bed when they came home. I agreed and we both got under the covers. She looked so much tinier in my parent's bed.

After a game of "I spy," we had a little chat about her tea party that she had had earlier that day. Every so often, she would lift her head up and look around the room. She wouldn't say anything; she would lie back down and snuggle her body against my side, under my arm. After she looked around the room a few more times without saying anything, I decided to ask her what she was looking at.

"Do you see something I don't?" I teased.

"No," she replied, but her eyes were still surveying my parent's room every few minutes.

"What are you looking at?" I asked.

"Nothing," she responded.

"Are you looking for something?" I tried to get an answer.

"Those mans don't talk, right?" she asked as she pointed all around the room.

"What men?" I asked as my eyes darted to every corner.

"Those mans," she pointed all around the room again.

Okay, I thought, *stay calm and don't scare Heidi*.

"You see men in mommy and daddy's room? You'd better tell them to go away!" I kidded as I tickled her, but Heidi shook her little head "no" and buried her head into my side.

"Do you want to play "I spy" again?" I asked.

"Sleep," was her reply. I thought about this for a few minutes and I truly believed that she saw something.

"I know!" I said. "Heidi, do you want to come and sleep in my bed?" I asked her.

"Yes!" she exclaimed, nearly hopping off of the oversized bed.

We raced to my bedroom, which made Heidi laugh so it put a smile on my face. Heidi and I snuggled together in my bed for a little while. It didn't take long for her to fall asleep. I fell asleep shortly after. I didn't hear my parents come in and Tommy must have slept all night, because Heidi and I woke up together in the morning with the sun shining on our faces.

Chapter 2

"Did you have a good time?" I asked my mother as Heidi and I came down the stairs together.

"We did, honey. Thank you for watching the kids. How was your night?" she asked. "Looks like you and Heidi had a slumber party," she added.

"Yeah, Heidi didn't want to sleep in her bed so I let her sleep in mine. Did Tommy wake up last night? I slept right through until morning. I didn't even hear you come in," I said to my mother.

"You were out cold when we came in and Heidi looked so comfortable in your arms so we didn't want to wake her. Tommy did sleep all night. Looks like you really tuckered them out," she smiled as she spoke.

"I didn't mind having Heidi in my bed," I smiled back at my mother. I made Heidi and I some toast. We sat together and ate our breakfast as my mother finished feeding Tommy.

After breakfast, I volunteered to clean up as I didn't have anything else to do. I was still upset about Jack and what had happened on Friday night. I was also concerned about the unexplainable episodes that kept happening in our house. Just in that week, I watched my sister's hair move by itself, I heard the same scream as my mother but in two separate areas of the house, and I witnessed my sister seeing what seemed to be spirits that I couldn't see. I had to talk to my parents about this but I didn't want to seem crazy. What was I supposed to do? Walk up to my mother and say "I think our house is haunted; I saw Heidi's hair move by itself"? She would have come up with explanations for everything that would seem believable but I know what I saw. I needed evidence and I promised myself that morning that I would get it.

I didn't talk to Emily all day because she went to church with her family on Sunday mornings. Then, they had brunch and spent the rest of the day doing family activities. I had so much on my mind and had to spend the day by myself. Emily would not have believed me any more than my parents would have. I would not have told her anything but at least she could have helped keep my mind off of the craziness in my house. I would have enjoyed the company. Jack and I didn't hang out on weekends so I couldn't count on him either. Besides, I was still upset with him. That Sunday went by really slowly.

*****

My parent's room was the coolest in the house and two out of the three things that had happened that week were in that room. I decided to wait until my mother was downstairs with my sister and brother, and my father was at work to pull out my camera. I set it up in the corner of my parent's room before I went to school on Monday. I really hoped to get some good footage when I got home from school.

Jack was standing in front of the school when Emily and I arrived. He was waiting for me.

"Hey Tina," he said with his eyes towards the ground. Hmmm, he was the shy one this time.

"Hey," I said in return.

"How was the rest of the dance? Did you have fun?" he asked. As if he could ask me that! Did he not remember what happened?

"No, I couldn't wait to leave. You really embarrassed me and you never even bothered to tell me what was going on," I said realizing too late how rude that was to say.

"I'm really sorry. It truly wasn't my intention to embarrass you. Pete should never have gone in to get you and I shouldn't have been there. I was just looking forward to seeing you at the dance all week that I couldn't stay away," he said all in one breath, again with his eyes glued to one spot on the ground. He was staring so intently that I had to look down to see if there was something there. There wasn't.

"You didn't tell me this before the dance; we could have gone together. Why didn't you just ask me to go with you?" I asked.

"I was afraid that you would say no." Again with his eyes aimed towards the ground. I fought the urge to look again.

"Are you ever going to tell me who that guy was that you were fighting?" I was dying to know.

"I'd rather not, if that's okay. It's a long story that I'm rather not proud of," he replied. *Then, why on earth would he bring him to the dance and want to see me all at the same time?* I wondered.

"Well, I can't force you to tell me anything, but I am curious about it all. You didn't come to school all day and then you show up at the dance covered in blood. You told me that he was the reason that you couldn't come to school that day but that's all you'll tell me," I rambled in hopes of getting some explanation.

"Maybe some other time?" he said looking drained. I felt horrible interrogating him. I had no intentions on even confronting him today.

"Okay. I'm sorry to pry; it's just seeing you in that state was really disturbing," I confessed.

"I'm sorry again," he apologized.

"For your information Jack, I would have most definitely said 'yes' if you would have asked me to go to the dance with you," I said smiling as I walked away to go inside with Emily.

I turned once to look at him and he was still standing in that same spot, looking down at the ground wearing a beautiful smile. I couldn't stop the butterflies from fluttering their wings in my belly because I was the reason for that smile.

Emily congratulated me as soon as we walked through the doors. "You finally said more than two words to him without giving me a signal to rescue you! I'm so proud," she said and pretended to wipe a tear from her cheek.

"He apologized for Friday night," I said. "He still won't tell me what happened though, he said 'maybe some other time,'" I said using my two fingers on each hand to sign quotation marks.

"Well, at least he is here today and he spoke to you and he gave you an apology," she said.

"I guess," was all I could say.

When the final bell rang, I was excited. I couldn't wait to get home to check my camera. If there was anything on it, I could finally show my parents and we could figure something out together.

When I came through our front door, Heidi was there to greet me. I covered her face with kisses and I told her that I would be back. I ran up the stairs and into my parent's room. I got my camera from the corner where I had left it and ran to my room. I closed and locked my door. I took a deep breath and closed my eyes. As much as I'd hoped that there was something to see on my camera, I was still petrified to see what it could be.

I sat on my bed and rested my back on a pillow that I propped up against the wall. I pressed the play button. I watched the footage for the first eight minutes before I realized that I could fast forward while still seeing everything. I was two hours into my recording and there was still nothing, just my parent's made up bed and nothing else. *Wait a minute,* I thought. I stopped fast forwarding and there it was. My parent's bed went from made to messy in just a few seconds. The top right hand corner of the comforter bunched up and it flew off the bed, landing on the floor. There was still the second blanket on the bed. A lump suddenly formed under the blanket, it looked as though someone was sleeping under it. It was moving up and down like it was breathing. I stared at the image on my small screen. I had to remind myself to breath. As fast as I could have ever imagined, the lump flattened and the comforter flew very quickly back onto the bed, making it look like it hadn't come off. The bed was made again.

I waited, staring for about ten seconds when out of nowhere two dark eyes appeared directly in front of my camera, staring at me. It backed up letting me see the rest of its face. Without any sound, it was screaming something. It was mad. It was screaming into the camera with no sound. It was there. It looked translucent, but you couldn't see through it; it looked like you should have been able to though. It was a dark shade but the background didn't show through. *It was mad at me*, was all I could think of, *I made it mad.*

I threw my camera onto my bed. I couldn't breathe. I tried to take deep breaths but they wouldn't come. I put my head in between my knees and tried again. Slowing my body started to accept my breaths of air. When I was able to breathe without thinking about every breath, I leaned back against the pillow on my wall and took deep breaths through my nose and out my mouth.

"Holy crap that is not what I expected!" I said out loud. I needed to hear something other than my own breathing. "That face looked so mean," I said out loud again. "Was he mad that I put the camera there?" I couldn't stop talking out loud to myself. I was so frightened.

I crawled off of my bed, grabbing my camera in the process. I was paranoid now, searching every corner of my room. I felt like someone was following me as I left my room and went down the stairs. I couldn't help but look over my shoulder every two seconds. When I stepped into the living room, my mother stopped playing with the kids and stared at me.

"Tina? What happened? You look as though you've seen a ghost!" she said as she got to her feet and came to stand in front of me. *Nice metaphor Mom*, I thought.

"I have to talk to you about something but not in front of the kids." I couldn't make eye contact as I spoke. I didn't know how to even start my explanation.

"Okay well, Dad will be home in just a few minutes. We can talk then," she decided.

I sat down and waited for my father. My mother sat down too but she was uneasy and wouldn't or couldn't stop staring at me. I could only imagine what was going on in her head. She probably thought that I was going to tell her that I was pregnant or moving out or something. My poor mother, I just couldn't tell her in front of Heidi and I couldn't stay upstairs any longer, I was too scared.

When my father arrived home, my mother didn't say anything. She simply stood up and took me by my hand and led me into the kitchen. My father just stood there, staring at us as we walked by him. He had a look of confusion on his face but he didn't ask any questions. My mother guided me to one of the kitchen chairs and took the one across from me. She didn't say anything; she just waited. I didn't know how to start.

"Okay, Mom. Strange things have been happening in our house that I'm not sure if you are aware of," I started.

Instantly, my mother's face softened. "Oh," was all she said. *Yep, she thought that I was pregnant.*

"Well, the night that I tried on some of your dresses and you and Heidi came up to see me in one of them, Heidi's hair was moving. I know what you're thinking, that there must be some explanation for it but I know what I saw. Her hair was being lifted by something. The ceiling fan was off and the window was closed. I wrote it off, Mom. I pretended that it never happened and I tried to forget it. Then, there was the scream that you and I both heard when I was taking a bath. Mom, I did not scream." I stopped for a second to see if my mother wanted to say anything, but she didn't. She sat and waited for me to finish. "Then, when you and Dad went to the wedding, Heidi wanted to sleep in your bed. We were lying in your bed when Heidi started to ask me about the men who don't talk that were in your room that night. I understand that she is only two but she was pointing at nothing and saying that she was pointing at the men!" I wanted my mother to say something now but she was lost for words. "Have you witnessed anything like that Mom?" I asked.

"No, honey, I haven't," she said. She looked confused.

"Today, before I went to school, after you made your bed and Dad went to work, I set my camera up in your room. I know it wasn't right, I should have asked first but I wanted to see if there was anything going on in your room." I pulled out my camera as I spoke. "I just watched this and it scared the crap out of me!" I exclaimed. "I would like you to watch it and then I would like to move!" I said as dramatically as I have ever said anything.

My mother smirked at my request to move, but she agreed to watch the footage. I pressed the button and was about to bring it to the second hour of the video when I noticed that there was nothing on the screen. I pressed the button again and there was nothing but a silent, static screen.

I looked at my mother and said, "It's gone." I didn't erase it. There is supposed to be an option to delete the videos and pictures and I didn't select "delete!" I didn't do anything! I started to cry. That was all I was able to do. My mother rushed around to my side and hugged me.

"You are tired, sweetheart. It's normal to put extra thought into the small stuff. Heidi is two. She has a great imagination and she is so smart for her age. You're in your last year of high school and you are stressed. I get it." She stopped and pursed her lips together for a second. "I know you're old enough to make your own decisions but I really think it would be a good idea to go to bed early tonight, get some sleep and start fresh tomorrow, honey," she was trying to comfort me.

"You don't believe me?" I said through my tears.

"I believe that you think you saw something. Of course I know you are not lying. But I also know that the last year of high school is stressful and stress plays a huge part in messing with people's minds," she said.

I knew she meant well. I smiled at her as I wiped my nose with the tissue that she had just offered me and I nodded my head in agreement. I didn't know what else to do. I had no evidence to back my story up. I got up and went to my room. I closed my door and put on some loud music. I placed my camera on my dresser and went to lie on my bed. I closed my eyes as I listened. My thoughts were everywhere. I was thinking of Jack and I was thinking of all the episodes that I had just brought up to my mother, trying to think logically. Of course, I didn't come up with anything. I thought about the footage on my camera and where it went. Then, it hit me. When something is deleted there is nothing there on the camera, but when I tried to show my mother, there was something there, it just turned into static. Did the ghost do that? Did it change my video to show nothing? Why would it only want me to see it? It's not like it wants my help, it looked so mean and mad. I shook my head in an attempt to rid my brain of any unwanted thoughts. I concentrated really hard on the lyrics to the songs that were playing.

I must have fallen asleep because when I came to, my room was silent and it was dark outside. I looked at my clock, 6pm. I got up and went downstairs. Everyone was just finishing supper.

"You're eating without me?" I nearly started to cry again as I asked. I was feeling vulnerable.

"Oh, honey, I went up to get you because your music was so loud that you didn't hear me calling your name. You were fast asleep so I turned off your stereo and let you be. I'm sorry if I hurt your feelings," my mother said. "I made you a plate." She got up to get it for me.

"It's okay, Mom. I didn't realize that I had fallen asleep. I was just confused. Sorry," I said and took my place at the dinner table to eat my food.

I was still feeling down when I went to school during the rest of that week. Emily was confused because I was talking to Jack every day and his full attention was on me. I couldn't tell her anything. I know what I saw, but I had no proof, and I didn't need someone else treating me like I was broken. My mother had been walking around me all week trying not to say anything that would "stress me out" and she had done the dishes every night so that I could "relax." I just wanted to be back to normal. The only time I smiled sincerely was when I spoke to Jack. When I was with him, even though it was only during the school breaks, I was happy and all my worries disappeared. At the beginning of every break, I hoped that he would ask me to be his girlfriend but he never did. I wasn't giving up though. I was confident that he would ask me soon enough.

*****

The following Saturday, Heidi came to me as I was watching TV in the living room and asked if I would play "ring around the rosy" with her. Of course I said "yes." I stood up and I took her left hand and when I reached for her right hand, she stepped back. I looked at her and smiled and I tried again, but again she stepped back.

"What are you doing? Do you want to play "ring around the rosy" or something else?" I asked.

"I want to play "ring around da rosy" but you keep forgetting Holly," she said.

"Oh, who's Holly?" I asked getting down on my knees to be face to face with Heidi.

"She lives in my room. She was allowed to play today," she said.

"Well, okay then, let's play!" I smiled and started to sing the song and turn in a circle holding only one of Heidi's hands with a gap on the other side of us.

Later on, when my mother was in the kitchen, I went in to ask her about Holly.

"Heidi has had Holly as her imaginary friend now for about two weeks," my mother said.

"Is that normal?" I asked.

"It's very normal, honey," she said reassuringly.

"She told me that Holly was allowed to play with her today. Why wouldn't she be allowed to?" I asked.

"Don't put too much thought into it, Tina. She is just an imaginary friend, that's all," my mother said with a note of finality.

Holly was all I heard about on Saturday. She played hide and seek, she liked all the same shows as Heidi did, she never stole any of Heidi's toys from her, and she was the perfect friend.

On Sunday, I decided that I wanted to ask Heidi about Holly. Maybe through my baby sister, I would get some answers as to what was going on in our house.

"Heidi, do you want to play "ring around the rosy?"" I asked.

"Yes!" she jumped with joy as she answered.

I took her left hand, and then reached for her right and she let me take it. We played two rounds before I asked her where Holly was today.

"She couldn't come down today. She was in trouble. She had a thing on her eyes and her mouth so she couldn't talk or see me. She was sitting on a chair in the corner." She was sad as she said this to me.

"Why was she being punished?" I asked.

Heidi shrugged her shoulders and went to finish her block castle that she was building earlier when I interrupted her to play. *That was disturbing*, I thought. Maybe Holly was a link to what I saw on my camera from my parent's room.

*****

Emily and I arrived at school later on that week. It had become a habit now that Jack would wait for me to get to the front of the school.

"Hey, what are you doing this Friday night?" Jack asked me as soon as I got within ten feet of him.

"Are you asking me out on a date Jack?" I kidded.

"Yeah, I am. Are you busy?" he asked. I laughed at his abrupt manner and told him that I was available. *Now this is exciting*, I thought.

*****

After school on Friday, I rushed home to get ready for my date. I forgot to tell my parents that I was busy that night, but when I got home, I told them and they didn't mind. I ran up to my room to get ready but when I reached the top of the stairs, I heard Heidi shouting at something from inside of her room. Her door was closed. This was very strange since my mother never let Heidi play upstairs alone, and it was never with the door closed.

"Leave me alone!!" she shouted. I approached the door and listened a little longer before interrupting her argument. "You're mean!" she shouted again.

I slowly opened her door and walked into her room. I stopped in my tracks because there was nobody there, not even Heidi. I scanned her room. I got on my hands and knees and looked under her bed. I opened her closet door and looked in, nothing.

"Is there anyone here?" I asked "Heidi, are you playing hide and seek?"

Nobody answered. I went to her bedroom door and walked out, closing the door behind me. Before going to my room, I went back downstairs to check on Heidi. I walked into the living room and there she was, colouring a picture on the floor, with Tommy beside her trying to take her crayons away.

"Were you colouring that picture for a long time? It's beautiful," I said to Heidi.

"Yes, it's for mommy," she replied.

"Well, you better hide it. I think mommy's trying to look at it!" I joked.

"Mommy! Don't see!" she said to my mother.

"I wasn't looking silly," my mother laughed.

I left the laughter in the living room and went back upstairs. I hoped that what I had heard was my imagination, but deep down I knew that it wasn't. I let it be though. I didn't want to dwell on it. I changed my clothes. I wasn't sure where we were going but I knew that Jack wasn't the "dress up to wine and dine" type of person. So, I just changed into a fresh pair of jeans with a purple top. I brushed my hair down to get rid of any knots and I redid my eye makeup. Before walking out of my room, I sprayed my perfume and walked through it. I never actually sprayed the perfume directly onto my skin. I didn't want anyone to notice the scent; I just wanted to be sure that I smelled clean.

Jack was at my door at five o'clock, just like he said he would be. I didn't invite him in. I gave my parents a kiss goodbye, promised to be home by my curfew and then walked out the door.

"Hey," he greeted me.

"Hi, where are we going?" I asked as I looked around for a ride of some sort.

"Where do you want to go? We can walk to get something to eat close by or if you want to go somewhere else we can call a cab," he said.

"No, let's walk. It's nice out," I said and I headed down my porch stairs.

We walked four blocks to a Chinese restaurant. It was one of my favourites. It was a buffet so we both grabbed our plates and filled them up. We had a wonderful dinner; the food was great and he was a gentleman. He even pulled my chair out for me.

After dinner, he wanted to take me to a movie. I wasn't so excited about that because I knew that he liked the scary ones and I can't stand to watch those kinds of movies. I didn't say anything though. I followed him out of the restaurant door and we walked towards the movie theatre.

"Do you know what movie you want to see?" he asked.

"Oh, you don't have one in mind?" I replied.

"I do, but I want you to choose our movie tonight," he said, then reached over and took my hand. I instantly entwined my fingers with his and a tingly feeling rose up my arm and down to my belly, which activated the butterflies. I blushed.

"Let's see what's playing and we can choose together," I suggested. He agreed and we walked in silence the rest of the way. We were both shy to hold one another's hand. It was sweet.

When we arrived at the theatre, there was a large selection of movies to watch. We broke it down to our top three choices and wrote them on a napkin that we found on one of the tables. We, then, bunched the three choices up into tiny balls and mixed them on the table. We both grabbed one leaving only one left. That was the movie we watched. It was a good movie. It wasn't a romance or a chick flick, but it wasn't a thriller or a horror movie either. It had a little bit of action and comedy all rolled into one. I enjoyed it, so did Jack.

After the movie, Jack walked me home, hand in hand.

"I was thinking a lot about us," he started, but without looking at me. He stared straight ahead. "I'm not sure how you feel about me but I really like you. I would really like if you'd be my girlfriend," he asked quietly. *I knew it.* I knew he would ask me tonight. I tried to hide my excitement.

"I would love to be your girlfriend," was all I said. I wanted to say, "Of course you dummy! It took you long enough to ask! It's about time you manned up!" but I didn't say any of that. He let my hand go and wrapped his arm around my shoulder and gave a little squeeze. Then, dropped his arm and took my hand again. My insides were screaming! I was so happy. I couldn't wait to call Emily.

When we arrived at my front door, I thanked him for our fantastic night and got up on my tip toes. I reached up to kiss him on the cheek. He let me but, as I started to back away, he put one finger on my chin and guided my lips to his. If my eyes had been opened, I'm sure that I would have seen the sparks fly. I was ecstatic. When we said goodbye for the eighth time, I climbed the stairs to my front door and went inside, two minutes before my curfew.

"I'm home," I said as I popped my head into the living room. "I'm going to bed, love you both!" I was giddy.

I called Emily as soon as I reached my room and told her everything. She was just as happy for me as I was. I hung up the phone and got ready for bed. *I have a boyfriend*, I thought to myself, *and it's Jack Hudson!* I wanted to dance or jump or scream. I had a hard time containing my emotions. I've liked him for so long!

I crawled into bed and thought about changing my style up a little for school on Monday. Now that I had a boyfriend, I should dress the part. But then, I thought, he liked me for me. I'm sure he wouldn't want me to change, so I chose not to stress about my clothes and went to sleep.

I woke up suddenly and looked at my clock, 2:42am. Then, something caught the corner of my eye. I turned my head slowly towards my doorway. It was dark but I made out the shape of a man. I stared for a second to be sure I was actually seeing someone.

When I realized I was, I asked, "Who are you?" He didn't answer but started to walk towards my bed. "Who are you?" I repeated as I sat and drew my knees up and hugged them against me.

He got to the foot of my bed and leaned down to rest both his hands on my bed. Fear ran through my veins and all I could do was stare. I was paralyzed with fear. He, then, started to crawl up my bed towards me. I hugged my knees closer and trembled. He stopped and looked up at me and smiled, a mean sadistic smile, before he faded into thin air. I watched him dissipate in front of my eyes. I was frightened and I still couldn't move. I wanted to turn my light on but my body refused to let me. I began to breathe through my nose and exhale through my mouth until my fear released me. I reached over and turned on my lamp. I lay my head back down onto my pillow but my eyes wouldn't close. My brain wouldn't let them. My eyes scanned all four walls and corners of my room for the rest of the night. I lay awake in my bed with my lamp on for the next four hours until I heard my mother's familiar voice telling me that it was time to get up.

Chapter 3

I was unable to sleep at night for the remainder of the week. I couldn't get the image of that man's face out of my head. It was horrible. I was able to get a couple hours of sleep here and there, mostly on the living room couch where I was surrounded by my family. When I went to bed at night, I refused to turn out my light. I would lie in my bed and stare at nothing. I tried reading a book or doing a crossword puzzle. I tried anything to help make the time go by. During that week, everyone asked me if I was okay, even the students who I rarely talked to. I knew that I needed sleep.

After a week of hardly sleeping and not seeing anything unusual, I decided to close my eyes. I slept the entire night without being disturbed or woken up.

In the morning, my mother woke me up to let me know that it was time to get ready for school. I rose, showered and got dressed. When I was finished, I went downstairs to join my family. My mother was preparing breakfast. Heidi was in the hallway; her entire body was pressed up against the wall, as far as it would go. She was crying and she was very scared. She noticed me when I walked in.

"Tina! Tina! Who is that man? I don't like him! Tina! Make him go away!" she screamed at me with her eyes shut tight.

I ran to her and picked her up. She clung to me and cried. I soothed her until she stopped crying and then I asked who she saw.

"He was mean, Tina! He was staring at me and was really close to me!"

I hugged her again and told her that it was okay and that he was gone. I brought her into the living room and looked into the kitchen where my mother and Tommy were. My mother was finishing up our breakfast. She didn't hear anything?

Heidi and I sat on the lazy boy and waited for breakfast to be ready when, out of nowhere, Heidi started laughing and threw her hands over her eyes and giggled loudly.

"What are you doing silly?" I asked her as I giggled as well. Her laugh was contagious. "I like that lady, Tina. She plays "peek a boo" with me!" she said as she clapped her hands in excitement.

"What lady?" I asked. The smile quickly disappeared from my face.

"That one!" she said pointing towards the stairway that led upstairs.

I was stunned and I got chills all over my body. I didn't want Heidi to see that I was scared, so I got up, holding out my arms, and asked if she wanted to see if mommy needed help in the kitchen. She agreed and I picked her up. As we walked to the kitchen, Heidi was saying "bye" to the lady. I really couldn't take it. I didn't want to be there anymore.

"Mom! Did you not hear Heidi freaking out in the hallway?" I demanded as I put Heidi down.

"No, are you okay Heidi?" she asked getting down on her knees to be at Heidi's level.

"There was a mean man near me mommy," Heidi replied. She continued, "But Tina helped me and the lady played "peek a boo" with me."

"Is that right sweetie?" my mother said to Heidi while eyeing me.

"Mom, you have to come to terms with the fact that this house isn't good. You're ignoring what I tell you because it's not normal, but Mom, even if it's not normal it's happening! I cried out to you and now Heidi is crying out to you. You have to listen..."

"Enough!" my mother yelled. "Tina, I cannot believe that you got your two year old sister to say something so horrible to try to get me to believe you!" she accused.

"What? I...." I stumbled on my words.

"I don't want to hear it, Tina!" my mother cut me off. "I don't want to hear any of it. If you so much as bring up another story about spirits in this house again, I will..." she was yelling at me.

"You will what Mom?" I challenged.

"Just never mind. I don't want any more talk like that in my house. End of discussion!" she said as she turned from me to get the breakfast plates.

"I'm not eating," I said and turned to leave. I grabbed my things for school and walked out of the house.

On my way to school, I thought about everything that's been going on in my house. I can't believe my mother thought that I would make Heidi lie. Why would I do that? Why would she think that? I was so frustrated. I decided that I would let Emily and Jack in on my secret. I wasn't sure how they would take it but I needed someone to talk to, someone who would believe me.

*****

"Do you believe in ghosts?" I blurted out as Emily, Jack and I ate our lunch. The table was empty except for the three of us. That's usually how it was.

"I never really thought about it," Jack said.

"I guess I do. I've never seen one though," said Emily.

"Well, I have and I do all the time. I have this man ghost in my house and he scares me. My sister saw him, but my Mom doesn't believe me." I was blurting everything out like they were my personal diary. "I videotaped him and he showed up on it and I saw him! When I brought my camera downstairs to show my Mom, all there was, was static!" I began to talk a little louder and noticed that I was when Jack and Emily started to look around as I spoke. I brought my voice down and continued. "I don't want to be at home anymore. I am too scared to close my eyes and go to sleep half the time, but I don't want to leave Heidi there to deal with the evil in my house with nobody there to believe her!" I said. I waited to see if they had anything to say.

"Do you see him a lot?" Emily asked.

"Just two times. I saw him in the camera and I saw him in my room. He was climbing in my bed but then he faded away," I admitted. I was so shy to say these things out loud. I would sound cuckoo if nobody believed me.

"Can he hurt you?" asked Jack.

"I don't know. I know that he can move and touch things. He played with my sister's hair, making her hair move up and down and side to side," I said, gesturing with my hands to emphasize the creepiness of what had happened.

"Well, that's freaky!" Emily said.

"I don't know if I believe in psychics but why don't you try one? Would that work?" asked Jack.

I shrugged my shoulders. At this point, anything was possible.

*****

We found a psychic medium that was able to come to my house. I knew my parents were taking the kids to my aunt and uncle's for supper and to play a few card games on Friday night. Therefore, I had a few hours alone at home. I scheduled the medium to come over to my house that Friday.

Emily and Jack met me at my place and we waited for the medium to show up. Her name was France and she was in her 50s. She had a thick French accent. She said she was sure to find out what was happening in our home.

When she came in, she winced and said the presence was really strong. We all sat down around the kitchen table. She took out a tape recorder and hit record. She was about to start the reading, when she stopped abruptly. She turned off the tape recorder and asked if she could walk around the house. Who was I to say no?

"Okay," I whispered. I was too scared to talk out loud.

France took some sage out of her bag along with a ceramic plate. She lit the sage and walked around the kitchen, fanning the smoke of the sage all around. With the three of us following her, she walked through the living room doing the same thing with the smoking sage. She went through the hallway and up the stairs. She went into my parent's room first. When she walked in, she stopped suddenly, leaving the three of us to bump into each other.

"Whose room might this be?" she asked without looking at me. I thought it was pretty obvious that it was my parent's room.

"It's my Mom and Dad's room," I whispered once again.

"A lot of things happen here, yes?" she asked.

"A couple of things that I've seen have happened in this room," I tried to talk louder but I couldn't. She heard me though.

"Hmmmm," was all she said. She continued to walk around my parent's room then out the door and into Tommy's room. She walked around fanning the sage going through each bedroom with the three of us trailing behind her. We made our way back downstairs and into the kitchen, where she explained what she had done. The sage was to calm the spirits down. She said that there was one in particular, a male, who was extremely upset. She told us what she had learned through her walk around the house.

"Long ago, there was a man, a woman and a child who lived here. The man was mean to the wife and daughter. He would not let the little girl go out of her room and when she did, it was for a short time and she needed..." she snapped her fingers twice while she remembered the word that she wanted to use, "...permission. She ate in her room and entertained herself most of the time. The wife, who was the little girl's mother, stayed with the little girl. The man murdered the wife and child and then himself. He did not want to go to jail. They've live here since then. They never left," she explained with so much emotion that I could picture the whole thing.

"Oh my God! Heidi has seen the little girl. We played "ring around the rosy" with her! Then, one day, Heidi said that the girl couldn't play because she had something over her eyes and her mouth. And she had to stay in the corner in Heidi's room; she wasn't allowed to play. Her name was Holly," I said sadly. "Heidi has seen the wife too. She played "peek a boo" with her!" I had goose bumps and I could no longer sit. I wanted to move away from this house, away from this man!

"We need to get the man to leave this home so the wife and daughter can leave and have peace," said France.

The three of us stared at her like she was crazy. She asked us to step outside so she could try to make him leave. She asked us to leave the door open. We did as she asked and waited outside. We could hear her yelling something that we couldn't understand and then we heard a struggle.

"Should we at least go in and check on her?" I asked.

"She said to stay outside. If we go in, we might ruin her whole process," said Jack wide eyed as he continued to listen.

Then, France emerged looking drained.

"He is gone but I'm sure he will be back. Tell the lady that she is free to go. Maybe she will leave faster if she hears it from you," she said as she walked towards her car. "Good luck." Those were her final words to me. *Good luck? Jeeze, did I really need luck?* I thought. *I just needed to move.*

We went back inside and noticed the intense smell of sage.

"Let's open some windows, especially in the bedrooms," I suggested. We all went around the house and did just that.

"That was crazy!" Jack said. "I hope it worked."

"Me too," I replied.

*****

The next few weeks were calm. There weren't any unusual activities. I was sleeping at night and smiling more. Jack and I had a strong relationship and it was growing. We no longer felt the need to talk to hide the silence, the silence was comfortable.

It was a Friday morning and I had just gotten out of the shower. I wrapped myself in my bath robe and turned the water on to brush my teeth. I was standing in front of the sink brushing my teeth, unable to see through my mirror since it was fogged up from my shower. Out of nowhere, I felt a hand on my lower back pressing me into the cabinet. *I thought I locked the bathroom door?* I wondered, as I pressed forward to let whoever in. Someone obviously needed to use the washroom right away, because my family always respected one another's privacy. I was still being pushed forward and I waited for them to squeeze through, which I understood because we had a small washroom, but it was taking a long time. Finally, I got annoyed and spun around to see who was taking so long and I faced an empty towel rack. There was nobody in the washroom. I looked at the washroom door and it was still locked. Fear struck me once again as I stood alone in the washroom waiting for someone to appear. Nobody appeared so I turned back towards the sink and quickly finished brushing my teeth.

When I was finished, I slowly wiped a streak through the fog in the mirror. Only my reflection was there. I blew out the air that I was holding in my lungs and turned to leave the washroom, when I felt a cool gust of wind across my face. I stopped and looked around but again there was nothing. I ran to my room and climbed under the covers, this time, not only to warm up but to also get the chill out of my bones.

*****

When I arrived at the corner to meet Emily, I was quiet. I was really upset to think that all that was going on in my house wasn't finished. I thought that the evil spirit had left. I accepted Jack's warm embrace when we arrived at the school. It was nice to have his arms around me, especially right now.

"He's back," I whispered to Jack.

"Did you see him?" he asked.

"No, I felt him. He was in the washroom with me this morning," I told him. I didn't want anyone to overhear me and think that I was crazy. Emily did overhear, and that was okay.

"Why don't we go to the library and check out the history on your house?" Emily asked.

I turned to look at her. "I never thought of that. We could see if we could get his name and maybe the name of the lady. We already know that the little girl's name was Holly," I said. "I think that's a great idea!" I told Emily.

We made plans to meet at the front of the school at the end of the day so we could all walk to the library together.

*****

When we arrived at the library, we headed for the old newspapers. Jack sat down and typed my address into the small computer.

"What year should I specify?" he asked looking up at me.

"I don't know. The only thing I know is the little girl's name," I said.

He tried writing my address and the name "Holly." A few headlines popped up. Jack read through those while Emily and I stood over him and waited.

"Here!" he said after fifteen minutes of searching. I leaned down and read "Double murder suicide." The address was mine and the names read "Arnold Trepherd, Amelia Trepherd and Holly Trepherd."

"Can you pull up the article? Or the Obituary?" I asked. I was excited, we were finally getting somewhere with this mystery.

"No, somebody checked it out. It says it's not available," Jack said as he read the details.

"How can somebody check out a newspaper clipping? That doesn't make any sense!" I said. "Someone stole it!" I accused.

"Look, there is a list of people's names who signed into this area. We were supposed to sign in when we got here. Let's see who the recent names are," Emily suggested. "Their security system isn't very good. We walked in without signing this thing!" she laughed.

We walked over to the list. The most recent person to sign in was my mother! We all stood up and looked at each other wide eyed. I had told Jack and Emily that my mother didn't believe me. I wondered if this meant that she did. A smile formed on my lips, maybe now we can talk about it and possibly move. That was all that was going through my mind at that moment.

"I will call you guys later, I'm going home. I need to talk to my Mom!" I was happy. I felt like I wasn't alone.

*****

"Mom!" I called as I walked in the door. "Are you home?"

"Yeah, I'm in the kitchen," she replied.

"Hey," I said as I walked into the kitchen. I started, "I just came back from the library with Emily and Jack."

"That's good, dear. Are you studying for a test?" she asked while she continued to cut some vegetables.

"We were in the newspaper section." She stopped cutting the veggies and looked at me as I continued. "We were trying to get information on this house and the people that lived here, but the article was missing." I took a breath and continued. "You were the last one to sign in to the newspaper area before us. I just need to know if you believe me now," I hoped.

"I did go to the library and I did look at the article. I want to believe you, I really do, but nothing that you say makes sense to me. I don't believe in the paranormal, I believe in the here and now," she sounded desperate for me to understand.

"Did you steal the article, Mom?" I asked.

"I had a feeling that you were going to go and do exactly what you did today and I didn't want you to see it. I didn't want you to put more nonsense in your head. I didn't think that you would see my signature. It was the last thing on my mind," she said. I thought about this for a second and I became angry.

"So, after seeing that the name of the little girl that Heidi plays with is the same name as the little girl who died here, you can't open up your little perfect box and try to believe me!" I shouted.

"I have never lied to you! I have never played games with you! I have never gotten into trouble. I'm always the goody two shoes who does nothing wrong, but the minute that I say something that doesn't make sense to you, I am all of a sudden tired and stressed! You took the time to go to the library and search for the history of this house but you still treat me like I'm crazy! Open up your eyes, Mom, and pay attention to what's going on around you!" I said as I finalized the conversation by walking out of the kitchen and going upstairs to my room.

I locked the door behind me. I should have asked her for the article but I was sure she would have never let me seen it.

A couple of hours later, while I was studying for my math class, I heard my mother on the other side of my door. She didn't knock but she slid something under my door. I walked over and looked at it. It was the article. I didn't open the door to thank her. I was still hurt that she thought that I would make this up. I sat and read the article:

"Deputies in Cornwall say a man gunned down his wife and their 3-year-old daughter before turning the gun on himself.

Police say Arnold Trepherd arrived at his home before dawn on Thursday. They believe Amelia Trepherd as well as Holly Trepherd are now dead, but they have yet to find the bodies.

County Sheriff Stan Chriffos confirmed that Arnold Trepherd, then, returned to their home in the quiet neighbourhood and turned the gun on himself."

I was crying when I stopped reading. I couldn't finish the article. I guess it didn't help to read it. All it did was give me a new fear and a name to go with the evil in this house.

I went down for supper and I didn't say much. My mother told me that my Aunt Nora was having a family get together on Saturday and asked if I'd like to join them. I declined. I thought that having the house to myself was perfect to have a movie night with Jack. I called Jack as soon as I had finished the dishes and invited him over for Saturday night. He said "yes" and that he was bringing the movie.

*****

My family left to go to the get together and I went to the kitchen to make some snacks for Jack and I. I popped popcorn, mixed some dip and pulled out the chips. I got a couple cans of pop. He was to show up at any minute. I went to my room and walked through a spray of perfume and grabbed a blanket. I brought the blanket down to the living room and sat on the couch and waited. The couch faced the picture window that leads to the road and our driveway, so I watched the road for a bit. The microwave beeped letting me know that the popcorn was ready. I went to the kitchen and emptied the popcorn into a bowl and did the same with the chips. I went back to the sofa and waited a little longer. I grew bored of waiting so I called Jack's cell. There was no answer; he must be on his way. I turned the TV on and I found a show that I liked and watched it while I waited. It was one of my favourites and I was in a good mood. I was very much looking forward to spending time alone with Jack. I laughed when the audience laughed and I tried Jack's phone again, still no answer. I called Emily after a while and talked to her as I continued to wait for Jack.

"It's been over an hour, Emily. Where could he be? He won't answer my calls," I complained.

"Maybe he's running late at home. Did you call his house?" she offered.

"No. Hang on. I will try with my cell," I told her. I pulled the house phone from my ear and put it on my lap and dialled Jack's home number on my cell. It rang five times and went to voice mail. "Voicemail," I said as I put the house phone back to my ear.

"I don't think he's going over, Tina. Do you want me to come and sit with you?" she asked.

"No thanks. I'm just gonna go to bed," I said as I sulked.

I hung up with Emily and went to the kitchen to put all the snacks away. When I was finished, I went to the living room and took one more glimpse outside. He still wasn't there so I closed the drapes. My cell phone rang, it was Jack.

"Hey," I said sweetly. "Where are you? Are you still coming over?" I asked in a flirty tone.

"You have some nerve!" He was angry? "I can't believe that you would cheat on me!" he yelled. "We're through! Do you understand me? I don't want to see you anymore, ever!" he yelled and he hung up the phone. What just happened? I was motionless, my mouth was gaping and I began to cry. I immediately called Emily and explained what happened.

"Holy! I wonder where he got his gossip from. Do you want me to call him? I can try to get his story and I could tell him that you've been waiting for him all night," she offered.

"Thanks Emily, I'd appreciate that," I replied. I needed to know what happened and what I did for him to think that I would cheat on him.

We hung up and again I waited. I sat at the end of the couch and leaned my head down on the arm and wept. Suddenly, I heard a loud breathing directly into my left ear. I turned quickly to see if someone was leaning over me but there was nobody there, the breathing was loud. I rubbed my hand against my ear and listened, the breathing was louder. *What the hell!* I thought. I placed both my hands over my ears and drew my knees up against my chest. I pressed my hands tight against my ears and squeezed my eyes closed. I stayed that way for a few minutes. I slowly unclenched my body and listened, the breathing was still in my ear! Was I going crazy? I stood up and walked in circles with my hands pressed against both sides of my head. I was freaking out. I was panicking and I couldn't calm myself down. The phone rang. I stopped walking and I let my ears go, the breathing was gone. I answered my phone. It was Emily. I calmed down.

"Hey," I answered. "Did you talk to him?"

"Yeah, I did," she said. "He claims that when he drove by your house, he saw you sitting on the couch with another guy."

"As if I would do that! Besides, I was waiting for him. If I was going to cheat, I would at least make sure he wouldn't catch me!" I shouted in return.

"Tina, did you hear me? He saw a guy sitting with you on the couch!" she repeated.

"I heard you! Do you think I'm lying? Do you believe him and not me? I was on the phone with you while I waited for him to show up!" I was defending myself at every different angle.

"He said that he took a picture of the two of you on your couch," she said.

"I'm gonna let you go and call him because this is insane!" I said and I hung up.

I dialled Jack's number and it rang three times before he picked up.

"Jack?" I said as soon as I heard the phone pick up on his end. He immediately hung up. *Oh, grow up*! I thought and I redialed.

69

"Jack! Don't hang up!" I shouted as I heard his end pick up again.

"What?" he replied coldly.

"Do you honestly think that I would cheat on you?" I asked.

"No, I didn't think that you ever would have, but I know what I saw," he replied coolly.

"Okay, Emily said that you have a picture of this guy and myself that you took. May I see it?" I asked.

"When?" he asked in return.

"Right now, of course. I will not sleep knowing that you think that I would do something like that to you and I also would like to know who the hell was in my house sharing my couch with me!" I shouted.

I finally convinced him to come over after a bit of coaxing. When he arrived, he knocked on my door and I let him in. I greeted him with a "hello" but he didn't reply. Instead, he looked around as if he was making sure we were alone.

"There wasn't anyone here nor is there someone here now, so you can stop acting like a jerk!" I said.

"It's the last picture that I took. Take a look," he said handing me the phone and I accepted it.

I scrolled to his pictures file and clicked on it. There was the thumbnail of my house. I opened the picture to let it grow to the entire size of the screen. I wasn't sure what I was about to see, so I prepared myself by taking a deep breath and exhaling. I looked. There I was sitting on the couch and right beside me was the mean man with the eyes. Holy crap! He looked as though he was watching TV with me and it looked like we were laughing together. I zoomed in to view only him. He was see through. I zoomed out and saw right away the difference in our looks. The picture of me and the background was vibrant, but he was dark and transparent. I looked at Jack who was staring at me with a smug look on his face, obviously mistaking my look of surprise with a look of guilt, and he was waiting for an apology.

"You idiot!" I yelled. I immediately drew back as those words left my lips. I was embarrassed to call him that, but it escaped my thoughts without warning. "Sorry, but did you look at this picture?" I asked.

"Only when I took it, why?" he asked curiously. I zoomed in and showed him what I saw. He couldn't deny it after seeing it. "I'm so sorry that I thought you were cheating on me!" he said as he hugged me. "I didn't want to look at the picture because I didn't want to see who the guy was. I just wanted it to show you in case you denied seeing somebody else! I'm so sorry, do you forgive me?" he asked.

"Of course I do!" I smiled at him. Then, I got a chill that travelled up and down my spine as I thought of something. The breathing! It was him!

Was he trying to tell me that Jack saw him or was he just trying to scare me?

Since Jack was over and he had his movie, we popped it in. I went to get all the snacks that I had just put away. We enjoyed our movie night nevertheless. We were very uneasy though, our eyes were everywhere except on the movie, searching the darkness for something that we didn't want to see.

Chapter 4

My parents weren't home yet when the movie finished. Jack and I were cuddled up on the couch, both of us feeling disappointed that the movie had to end. We pulled away from each other and I got up to put his movie back in the case.

"I was hoping my parents would be home by now because I wanted to show them your picture. Can you text it to me please?" I asked.

"Sure," he replied, and he found the picture and sent it to me. My phone notified me right away; I could hear it from the other room.

"Thanks," I told him.

"I guess I will take off then and let you get some sleep. I am so sorry for thinking that you would cheat on me. I should have looked closer at the picture. I feel so stupid," he said.

"Don't worry about it. We are fine, we figured it out and we are still together. No worries," I smiled.

"Together forever," he replied as he leaned down to kiss me. The sparks flew and my butterflies went wild as I memorized every second of our kiss so I could store them in my memory bank forever. His arms wrapped around my body perfectly and I was truly comfortable. We stopped when we heard the car doors slam from my driveway.

"My parents are home," I stated the obvious.

"Okay, I will call you in the morning," he said with a smile and gave me one more lingering kiss on my forehead. I closed my eyes and savored it.

He walked out the door as my family walked in. I went to my purse and pulled out my phone. I scrolled through my text messages and saw the text from Jack. *Good*, I thought, *it's there*. I clicked on the picture to make it bigger and I suddenly grew faint. I sat on the closest spot available, which was the couch, and I stared at the picture. In it, I was sitting alone on the couch, laughing by myself at the TV. The man wasn't there.

"What's the matter, honey?" my mother asked. "You look sick."

"I'm fine," I said. I got up and walked to the stairway to go up to my room. It's not like she'd believe me anyway. I closed and locked my door when I got to my room, and I checked my phone again. I pulled up the picture and again it was only a picture of me. *What's going on?* I asked myself. *Does he want to be seen or does he not want to be seen?*

I stripped down to nothing and put on my robe. I went to the washroom and made sure to lock my door. I turned the shower on and tested the water from the outside of the bathtub. I got in and let the water soak me. I was in the middle of washing my face when I felt like I needed to open my eyes. I got an eerie feeling that someone was watching me. I hurried to get the soap out of my eyes so I could see. I managed to get one of my eyes rinsed out enough to open it. There was nobody in the shower with me. I looked across the shower curtain, it looked fine. My eyes traveled to the crease of the curtain against the wall. I didn't notice anything so I grabbed it and pulled it open. Nothing. I released the air that I was holding in and closed the shower curtain. I closed my eyes and brought my head up to wet my hair. I got that eerie feeling again so I opened my eyes and looked up. I screamed without telling myself to; it came out without permission and it wouldn't stop. Staring at me from over the curtain were the eyes of death. They were grey and black, the same ones that were in my video. My brain wouldn't let me stop screaming but it wouldn't let me move either. I stood and screamed as I stared back at the gruesome eyes that were staring at me. I looked away for what seemed like a second and, when I looked back, he was gone. I stopped screaming and I heard a laugh, a mean laugh that faded to nothing. I waited for a second before I peered out. He was gone. I took a second to compose myself. My parents were both banging on the washroom door, yelling through the cracks to see if I was okay.

"I'm alright, I just spooked myself. I'm sorry to have scared you," I yelled. I heard their sighs of relief and annoyance as I answered them.

"That girl really needs to sleep," I heard my mother tell my father as they descended the stairs.

I climbed back into the shower and quickly finished rinsing myself off. I got out and went to my room, and had yet another sleepless night.

When it was morning, I put my house coat on and went downstairs for breakfast. It was Saturday so I was in slow motion to get ready for the day. When I entered the kitchen, my mother was preparing a quick breakfast for my brother and sister so I poured myself some cereal.

"Mom, can I ask you something without you getting mad at me?" I asked.

"You can try but I won't guarantee that I won't be upset," she replied honestly.

"I was just wondering why you decided to let me read the article the other day," I said.

"What do you mean? You said the article wasn't at the library." She looked puzzled.

"Yeah, because you took it but then you gave it to me," I reminded her.

"I never had it. I went to the library to look up the history but I never said that I took the article," she replied.

"You said you were afraid that I would have crazy thoughts or whatever so you took it so I wouldn't see it," I said.

"No, honey, it's still at the library I'm sure," she said.

"But you slid it under my door the day that

we fought about it," I said with a note of uncertainty in my voice.

"Tina, honey, I did not slide anything under your door, sweetheart," she said.

"Do you want me to show it to you?" I asked.

"No, that's okay," my mother replied.

"I want to show you. I will be right back." I put my spoon in my bowl of cereal and ran upstairs to get the article.

I opened my desk drawer that I had stored it in and it wasn't there. I rummaged through it and it didn't show up. I opened the other drawers and there was nothing there either. This is impossible. Why are all these things happening to me? The ghost obviously doesn't want us living here anymore but refuses to let me show my mother the evidence that he exists. I began throwing things in my search for the article. My mother quietly showed up at my door, leaned against the frame and waited for my fit to end.

"It was here Mom and you slid it under my door, I know you did," I accused.

"I did no such thing. I didn't take the article home," she said.

I heard someone whisper in my ear. I couldn't make out what was said; it sounded like ~*it was me*~

"What?" I asked. I didn't know where the whisper came from. I spun my head and looked around my room. Nobody was behind me.

~it was me~ There it was again! A whisper saying it was them. *Oh! Could it be him?* I thought. My mother was staring at me with a confused look. I guess I looked a little crazy.

"What is it, dear?" she asked.

"Nothing, I'm just sorting things out in my head. I'm trying to remember where I put that darn piece of paper," I said.

"We will worry about it later, dear. Come finish your breakfast," she said as she guided me down the stairs.

*****

On Sunday, I still hadn't found the paper and the library was closed. I made a promise to myself to go to the library the next day after school and see about that article. I was in my room relaxing and reading a book in the afternoon when I heard someone breathing in my ear again. I looked over, startled, to see that nobody was there. This time, I chose to ignore it. I thought if maybe I didn't make a scene, he would leave me alone. I continued to read without an expression on my face. But the breathing grew louder. I set my book down and walked over to my desk. I grabbed my school work and started to go through it. He wasn't giving up and I was having a hard time ignoring him. I held my cool and kept a straight face in hopes that he would think that I couldn't hear him.

After answering a few questions in my

homework, I closed my book because I was unable to concentrate and went downstairs. He followed me. My mother was watching a show so I sat down beside her. At this point, I imagined he was growing frustrated at my lack of annoyance because he was become extremely loud in my ear. I asked my mother what she was watching and she answered. I couldn't hear her over the breathing. I asked again a little louder this time. She looked at me, creased her eyebrows and repeated the name of the show.

I still couldn't hear her, so I shouted, "What?"

My mother then stood up and stared down at me with a puzzled looked. She asked me a question but all I heard was his darn breathing and it was echoing through my head, it was entering in both my ears. I sunk into the couch and told my mother that I had a headache. She went to the kitchen to get me some medication. I tried to decline it but she insisted. I guess my facial expression had pain written all over it, except she didn't understand the pain that I was actually in. He was breathing so loudly and it was giving me a headache anyway, so I took the pills and went back up to my bed. I lied down on my side with one ear pressed against my mattress and I pressed a pillow on top of my head against my other ear. It worked! *Now all I had to do was stay like this forever*, I thought gloomily. I wasn't sure what to do. I fell asleep for a bit but woke up shortly after because I let my pillow go and his breathing woke me up. I sat up and decided to try going outside. I went downstairs and put my coat on. I shouted over to my mother that I was going for a walk. She again looked at me with the strangest look; I guess I shouted a little too loudly again.

I got outside and the breathing stopped, thank goodness. I relaxed my body; I hadn't realized that I was clenching all my muscles as he was irritating me with his breathing. I started to walk. I decided to just take a walk around the block and go back home. If the breathing happened again, I would go outside and sit on my porch, because the breathing had stopped as soon as I closed my front door. I shoved my hands in my pockets and I began to walk. I had a sense that someone was coming up fast behind me so I moved over to the side to give room for them to pass me. I didn't get passed by anyone but the feeling was still there so I looked behind me; nobody was there, but he found me. The breathing started again. He was right in my ear. I tried walking faster but he kept up with me. I starting jogging so I could get home faster and his breathing became louder. Tears of fear and frustration began to fall down my face.

When I arrived home, my mother greeted me at the door. I made out, through the breathing, her asking me if I was okay. I told her that my headache was still really bad and I went back to my room. I searched through my school bag for my

MP3 player and shoved the headphones in my ears. It worked. I left them in and played around with the volume. I brought the volume down as low as it would go before I heard his breathing and then brought it up one notch. I still had a hard time hearing the noises around me but it was better than his breathing.

I went back downstairs, sat on the couch and stared at the TV. I couldn't hear what they were saying but I still watched. I could feel my mother's eyes on me but I didn't feel like explaining nor did I know how to explain, so I kept my eyes forward. Then, I felt her shaking me and she yelled at me to turn down my music because she could hear it over her show. I tried but his breathing seeped through the music so I got up and went to the kitchen. I made myself a snack and ate it in there. I didn't know what to do. I annoyed my mother with my music in the living room, my snack was done in the kitchen and I didn't feel like going back to my room. I couldn't call anyone because I couldn't hear. Forget it; I went back up to my room. I laid on my bed and stared at the walls until I grew bored and fell asleep. It was dark when I woke up. I looked at the clock it was three am. My music was still going. I pulled out one earphone and the breathing was still there. *Holy crap*, I thought as I shoved the earphone back in, *give it up already*! I laid back down and fell asleep.

I woke up in the morning when my mother shook me awake, again with the puzzled look.

"Why are you still listening to music?" I heard her faintly through the breathing and the music.

"It helped me sleep," I replied.

"Are you going to take them out?" she asked.

"Not right now," I said.

I did need to take them out because my battery was almost dead. I looked up at my mother who, staring at me, waited for me to turn my music off. I rolled my eyes and pulled the earphones out of my ears trying to look normal in front of her. She didn't buy it, but at least she walked out of my room. I hurriedly plugged my MP3 player in to charge and I took a shower. After my shower, I quickly got dressed, put my hair in a wet ponytail and jammed by earphones back in my ears. I skipped breakfast and left the house.

I waited at the corner that Emily and I met at every day. I sat on the curb for twenty-five minutes until she showed up. She asked me about my earphones and I told her that I was comfortable with them in. She left it at that, thank goodness. I went to my first period class; it was math. I turned down the volume as low as I could but Mr. Walsh sternly told me to turn off my music. I tried turning it down lower but I didn't fool him.

"Ms. Trudent! If you do not take your earphones out of your ears, I will ask you to leave. Be careful Ms. Trudent, this is a very important year, and you do not want to make any mistakes," he threatened.

I took my earphones out and the breathing swallowed me whole. It felt like it was in surround sound. I clamped my hands over my ears, shrunk down into my desk and squeezed my eyes closed. I drew a lot of unwanted attention.

"Ms. Trudent, what is the matter? You are once again disturbing my class," Mr. Walsh sternly asked.

"May I be excused? I have a migraine," I lied.

"You may. Have you thought that maybe it could be that music that gave you a headache? Hmmmm," he commented. I nodded my head and left the classroom as quickly as I could. I put my earphones back in and turned my music up really loud. I walked back home.

When I arrived home, I went directly to my room. I wasn't sure if my mother had noticed or said anything, because my music was blaring in my eardrums. I took off my jeans and got under my covers. I did not close my door. I left it open for my mother in case she needed me and if I didn't hear her calling or knocking on my door. I closed my eyes and fell asleep. I woke up in the early afternoon because my MP3's battery had died and the breathing was awful. I didn't have the energy to walk over to my desk to plug it in so I took the earphones out of my ears and squeezed the pillow over my head. I stayed like that for hours, not able to fall back to sleep. My mother came in to check on me and I told her that I still had a migraine. She left me be.

After supper, that I did not eat, Emily came to visit me. My mother let her in. She came to my room but I refused to take the pillow off of my ear, so I apologized and told her that my head was too sore to even talk. She left. I felt bad not telling anyone what was happening but it was even too crazy for me to believe. My mother came up a little while later with the phone; it was Jack.

"Hey, you weren't at school today. Are you okay?" he asked.

"No, my head really hurts. It's really hard for me to talk right now," I explained.

"Oh, do you want me to let you go?" he offered.

"I do but I don't want you to be upset. It hurts to even have my eyes open. I'm really sorry but I will call you as soon as I feel better," I said and we hung up.

I fell back to sleep with my pillow over my ear and I didn't wake up until morning. When I woke up, my body was so stiff that it felt like I didn't sleep at all. I got up and plugged my MP3 in and went back to bed. I was afraid that my mother would admit me into the psychiatric unit at the hospital but I couldn't help it. I chose to stay in bed for the day again. I didn't know what else to do or how to handle this. My mother was worried; she kept coming upstairs to check up on me. I stayed in my bed all day. My mother brought me food and drinks every couple of hours. It felt like the day would never end, but it did. I heard my family wishing each other a good night and getting ready for bed. I got into position with my pillow over my head and went back to sleep.

The next morning, I chose to go downstairs for a bit. I sat on the couch and did my best to ignore the breathing. Heidi was playing; she was having a tea party. She poured herself a cup of tea and another one right across from her. She sat and sipped her pretend tea, and stared at the empty chair. She was having a conversation that I couldn't make out over the breathing. Suddenly, the breathing stopped and Heidi turned her head towards the stairway to listen. I sat forward to watch her. She looked at me with her little eyebrows up high like she was questioning something. Then, she looked back at the stairway.

"What is it Heidi?" I asked.

"Who said my name?" she asked in return.

"You heard someone say your name? Was it a man's voice like Daddy's or a lady's voice like Mommy's?" I questioned.

"It was a man," she said.

"What did he say?" I pressed for information.

"Heiiiii-diiiiii," she said in a creepy voice. It was quiet in my head. I went closer to Heidi and knelt beside her.

"Have you heard this voice before?" I asked.

"No," she said with no concern as she continued with her tea party.

I didn't try for more information. I called over to the kitchen to tell my mother that I was going to get ready for school, so she knew that Heidi needed supervision. I looked around as I walked to the stairway. I was shivering out of fear that the breathing would come again. I hoped and wished that it wouldn't. I was cautious of every step I took and what I did. I didn't want to upset him and have him do that to me again. I showered and got dressed for school. I knew that I was going to be late but it was better than missing another full day.

*****

By the time the weekend started, I was still free from hearing the breathing in my ears. I had made plans to go out with Jack, Emily and a guy that Emily was interested in, Joel. We decided on a night club called "Jupiter's." It was designed for teens so there wasn't any alcohol; it was just dancing, food and soft drinks.

Jack and I met at Emily's house before going to the club because she was too shy to meet up with Joel by herself. The three of us then headed over to Jupiter's to meet Joel and have some fun.

We found a table and got comfortable. Joel found us and we ordered some snacks and sodas.

Emily and I danced while we waited for our munchie platters to arrive. We were having a great time. We were laughing, dancing and eating some great greasy food. After a bit, Joel leaned across the table and asked Jack about the fight that broke out at the school a few weeks ago. I remembered that fight very clearly but I never brought it up to Jack and I still never knew why there was a fight in the first place, so my attention spiked up.

"Dude, it's all good. I haven't seen that guy since," Jack told him.

"Yeah but what happened for the fight to start?" Joel asked.

"It was all a huge misunderstanding," Jack said. He was avoiding the question.

"Hmmm, well it had to be something crazy because the two of you looked as though you were about to kill each other." Joel wasn't giving up.

"Let's drop it okay? Let's have fun," Jack said.

"I wouldn't mind knowing what happened either," I said.

"Holy crap! What is this? Interrogate Jack day?" he yelled as he stood up.

I brought my eyes down and stared at the table. He walked away. I looked up at Emily and she was speechless. Joel just looked confused. I watched as Jack walked away; it didn't take long before he was out of sight. When he came back a few minutes later, he put his arm around me and apologized to all of us. He took a deep breath before he explained what happened that day.

"That morning, I was walking to school when I was stopped by three guys in a car; they asked me to do them a favor. I told them that I didn't know them so why should I, right?" He looked at us for approval, so the three of us silently nodded our heads in agreement. "So I kept walking. They told me that I would get paid five hundred dollars to deliver a package for them. The destination wasn't far so I stopped walking and listened to them. All I had to do was put the package in my book bag, walk about six blocks, knock on the door of the address they gave me and hand the guy the package. When the guy opened the package, he was to give me the money. Sounded easy enough so I agreed to do it." He again looked up for our nods of approval, but he didn't get them this time. He continued his story anyway. "I put the package in my book bag like I was instructed to do and I started walking. The car took off; spinning its tires and not a second later the police were on their tail. I got nervous, realizing that I could go to jail depending on what I was carrying. I kept calm though and walked faster. A few minutes later, the police were pulled over beside me and asked me if they could look in my bag. I did as they said and after they opened the package, they arrested me. I spent the day in the police station defending myself. They let me go only when my parents came to pick me up." He stopped and looked at us, and then continued. "I promised myself that I would make my first move with you that night so I walked over to the school. On the way there, those guys found me and beat the snot out of me for getting caught. They followed me to school and you all saw the rest."

He looked at us all, one at time, with his eyebrows raised to see if we were satisfied. We were. I didn't know what happened that day but that's not what I had expected. After a moment of not saying anything, the four of us got up to dance. We had fun and we continued to have fun until the club closed. Emily decided to let Joel walk her home, and Jack and I walked to my house hand in hand. When we arrived, we both knew that it was too late for him to visit so he gave me one of his long, beautiful kisses outside on my doorstep. After a few failed attempts on saying goodnight, I finally broke free of his embrace and went into my house for the night. I was still laughing when I peeked at him through the window. He was standing there with a beautiful smile on his face and he waved goodnight.

I climbed the stairs to my room. The house was quiet; everyone was sleeping. I crawled into my bed and quickly, happily fell asleep.

*****

When I woke up the next morning, I felt like I was pressed up against the wall, like there was someone there lying beside me. I looked over and of course I was alone, but I could see a groove in the pillow next to me in the shape of a head. I sat up and stared at the pillow making sure that it wasn't sleep causing me to see this. I yelled for my mother to come into the room.

When she got to my room, I was still sitting on my bed with my legs crossed and my back against the wall.

"What is it, honey?" she asked.

"Look at my pillow, Mom, do you see a groove like someone is laying on my bed?" I asked her.

She looked down and I saw the recognition in her eyes. She saw what I was seeing. Hope rose up and through my body as I knew she saw the spirit that haunted me. She stared for a few seconds before she composed herself and told me that it was probably because I was sleeping in that spot all night. I know she saw the groove and what it meant; her eyes gave it away. Just as I started to protest, her eyes went back to the pillow as if something caught her attention, so I looked at it as well and I saw the pillow slowly fill out and go back to normal. It looked like someone got up from that spot. I looked back up to my mother. She crossed her arms.

"There, see? You must have slept on it and it's just now taking back its form."

"Seriously, Mom? Do you believe what you are saying? You just saw what I saw and you know that these pillows don't form to our heads!" I replied.

"What are you trying to say, Tina? That there was a ghost sleeping beside you?" she laughed uneasily.

"Yes, that's exactly what I'm trying to say!" I said.

"Well that's ridiculous," she said. "Come and have some breakfast." She dismissed our conversation and walked out of my room.

Downstairs, everyone had started their morning. My mother was in the kitchen cooking food, my father was on the computer, Heidi was watching her favourite TV show and my brother was drinking his bottle in his high chair waiting for his breakfast. I sat on the couch with Heidi and watched "The Silly Rabbit" show with her. She laughed so hard watching this show that it made me laugh.

While Heidi and I sat together laughing, I caught something in the corner of my eye. I looked towards the staircase and saw a woman; she was standing there looking down at the floor. She was wearing a long light blue dress, she was bare foot and her hair was long, wavy and light brown. I sat and stared at this woman as she began walking towards the living room. She kept her head down. She walked by us and walked straight through to the kitchen. She circled the kitchen table and came back to the living room. She stopped in front of the TV, facing the TV, but her head was still tilted towards the floor. If I really wanted to continue watching the program, I could have watched it through her, but I was fascinated by this beautiful woman. She slowly turned around, still looking at the floor, then slowly she brought her head up and her eyes met mine. She stood and stared and I couldn't break the connection, I stared back. She slowly walked towards me; I didn't move. When she was about three feet away from me, she swiftly bent down and brought her face just inches from my own. She startled me and I jumped. I'm not sure if Heidi or anyone else noticed but we continued to stare at each other. I couldn't look away. Out of nowhere, she began to cry; she wasn't sobbing, she was just crying. Still staring back at her, I watched as silent tears fell from her eyes, onto her cheeks and they would have landed on my lap had they been real. I looked down at my hands that I had resting on my lap to see if there were tears falling on them. My hands were dry. I looked back up and I got locked back into her stare. She continued to cry when I suddenly started crying and I couldn't help it. I cried silently at first, and then my crying slowly turned into sobbing and gasping for air. I reached out to hug her, to console her but she disappeared. She vanished out of thin air. When I came back to reality, my entire family, my mother, my father and my sister, were all standing in front of me, staring at me with looks of confusion and fear. I looked at them and I became angry at their stares.

"Did you not see the woman who was

standing in front of me crying?" I screamed at them. They all shook their heads "no."

"Well, she was there and she was crying and so I started to cry because I could feel her emotions, I could feel her sadness!" I didn't know how to explain the sadness because I was confused. I was scared. I had so many things running through my mind at that moment that I began to cry harder and louder.

"What's wrong with me? Why can I see spirits that all of you can't? What did I do to be the one to be going through this? No one believes me; you all look at me like I'm crazy!" I started to lash out at my family, but my mother came to me and she hugged me until I stopped crying. She didn't say that she believed me, but I knew that she at least understood me.

*****

When I woke up the next morning, I was drained. I was emptied of all my emotions. I rolled out of bed and went through the motions of getting myself ready for the day. I couldn't shake the horrible feeling. I felt like I was losing my mind but I knew that I wasn't. I knew that I needed to help this woman and her daughter. But how? What can scared little me do to help get rid of this ridiculously mean man?

I thought about this all day while I was counting down the hours of my dull Sunday; I was beginning to love dull days. I thought about calling France back, our trusty medium who had once made Arnold leave, but this time I would beg the woman and her daughter to get out. I won't let them miss their chance. I read somewhere that if you tell them to go towards the light that they will go on to heaven; I will do that! I will tell them to get out and go towards the light.

I called Jack and told him what I had experienced with the beautiful lady the day before and all about my new idea. He was all for it. We just had to wait for my parents to leave again for a few hours. Later, I called France and made special arrangements with her so that she could come on short notice. My parents usually leave at night and she does most of her readings during the day, so she agreed.

I went to bed that night with a little bit of satisfaction flowing through me. My parents were eyeing me all day waiting for me to break down again. I'm sure that I kept my composure. I wished them both a good night and went up to my room. I've been sleeping with my door open lately in hopes that if something happens, my parents would have more of a chance of witnessing it.

I went to sleep pretty easily but was woken when I heard my door slowly close. I sat up and tried to make sense of what was happening; my brain was too tired to think. I laid back down and reached for my light to turn it on, when the most beautiful angelic voice stopped me and asked me to help.

"Please, Tina, help my Mom and me...." she said.

Assuming it was Holly, I answered her, "I'm going to do my best, sweetheart, just stay away from him!"

She gave me a sweet little laugh and thanked me as she opened my door and left. All was quiet. I stared into the hallway in hopes of getting a glimpse of the sweet girl, but nobody was there.

I tried hard to fall asleep but my mind continued to wonder what the mom and her daughter were doing. Were they hiding in a corner together? Were they acting like a family in hopes to not make Arnold mad? Was Holly hoping for a day of play? It was so sad for me to think about but I stayed awake until morning, praying and hoping that I could make things right.

*****

"You're coming with us!" my mother yelled when I refused to follow them to my aunt's on Tuesday night.

"I don't want you staying home alone. I don't believe that you will be okay!" she continued.

"You don't believe that I will be okay?" I repeated and smirked. "Why not? Are you afraid the monsters might get me or are you afraid that I might get myself?" I retorted. I knew that she was afraid that I might hurt myself but I was too scared to hurt myself. I was too scared of everything.

"Stop being dramatic and get ready. Aunt Nora hasn't seen you in a while and she misses you. I want you to come, so get ready... Now!" she ordered. I knew I was defeated so I turned around and marched up the stairs to get ready.

*****

"How is school, Tina?" my uncle Mike asked as I pushed my mashed potatoes around with my fork.

"Good," I said without looking up. I could sense them all looking at each other with questions in their eyes. I was always so polite but I couldn't bring myself to care. "Hey!" I exclaimed as I looked up at everyone. "Do you believe in ghosts? Like the ones that haunt houses because they either don't want you there or they need your help?" I blurted out.

I looked around, everyone had stopped eating. My father's mouth was open, my aunt and uncle were staring at me with their forks full and midway to their mouths, and my mother dropped her fork. Thankfully, my mother fed Heidi earlier so she was playing in the living room and didn't hear anything.

"What?" I asked. "It's just a question." Holy! And they call me dramatic. "Do you?" I pressed.

My aunt answered first with an "I'm not

sure," my uncle didn't say anything, and my parents just stared at me.

"I do. Our house is haunted. I've seen two ghosts and I heard one because she spoke to me. Heidi? Yeah, Heidi also sees them but nobody believes me... Do you Aunt Nora? How about you Uncle Mike?" I was so bold but I couldn't help it. My parents were stumbling on their words trying to explain that I wasn't sleeping properly and that I've been getting migraines. It was my turn to stare at them like they were crazy. Do they realize how stupid they sound?

We managed to get through supper; it was horrible. At the end of the night, I apologized to my aunt and uncle as did my parents and we got into the car. I was ready. I was ready for the yelling and being accused of trying to embarrass them because they wouldn't let me stay home, but they didn't say anything. We drove home in silence.

When we arrived, my father pulled into the driveway. I gathered up my brother's diaper bag and some loose toys. I unbuckled my sister and we walked to the front door and waited for my parents. They had my brother and some leftovers from supper. I moved out of the way so my father could unlock the door. I was desperate for them to say something to me, even if they yelled at me, but they said nothing.

As my father opened the door, he gasped, froze and stared. I let go of Heidi's hand and peeked through the door. The entire kitchen was inside out. All the cupboards were open and the dishes, pots and pans were on the floor. Most were broken. All the drawers were open and the silverware on the floor. The refrigerator and freezer doors were wide open with all the contents spilled onto the floor, all spoiled. The food from the cupboards was lying on the floor. The boxes were crushed and the cans were dented. My father managed to step inside so I squeezed by him. I ran into the living room; it was perfect. I went upstairs and through the house and all that was destroyed was the kitchen. I checked the door and it was still locked and intact. I ran back upstairs to check that all the windows were closed; they were. I did the same downstairs and there were no signs of a break-in. I went back to the kitchen without saying anything; my father sped by me and checked the house. I knew that even if I told him that I had checked, he'd still want to look. He came back down and confirmed that the rest of the house was untouched. My mother was on the floor picking up the broken dishes when she said that maybe the robber heard us coming.

"Mom, all the doors were locked," I said quietly. She glared at me.

"Maybe they used a window," she said through clenched teeth. Wow, okay. I wasn't saying anything else.

I picked up Tommy, took Heidi's hand and guided her into the living room. I put Tommy down into his seat and turned on the TV. When the kids were settled, I went back into the kitchen to help my parents clean up. It was quiet; nobody said anything as we cleaned.

I was the first to run upstairs and jump into the shower after cleaning the kitchen. When I was finished, I didn't go back downstairs. I went straight to my room and closed the door. I stood against my door with my forehead pressed against it for just a second.

"What a night," I whispered to myself. I heard a chuckle from behind me. I spun around and there sitting in my chair was Arnold. He had his legs crossed with his elbows resting on his knees and his intertwined fingers under his chin while he stared at me.

I froze in place but I didn't break the stare. He stared at me for a little longer then he looked down and shook his head as he muttered, "Pathetic." He looked up at me before he disappeared.

It didn't take long before I regained my composure; I didn't dwell on his appearance. I crawled into bed and fell quickly to sleep.

The trees surrounded me but I managed to run by each one without stopping or hitting any. I looked back and I didn't see him anymore. *I've outrun him*, I thought. I stopped for a second to breathe and to take in my surroundings but, before I could do that, I heard a branch snap and the sound of dry leaves crumbling. I looked back and there he was running full force towards me. I exhaled and I ran. I ran with every ounce of energy I could find, when suddenly I fell. I tripped over a root that stuck up from the ground and I landed face first into the muddy path. I tried to stand but my legs wouldn't work. I tried to scream but nothing came out. I looked behind me and there he was. Arnold stood above me, for just a second, before he reached down to grab me.

It wasn't long before I woke up, drenched in sweat.

Chapter 5

Waking up after having a dream of Arnold chasing me was terrifying. I sat up in my bed and wiped the sweat dripping from my forehead with my top sheet. I took a second before standing. When I was breathing normally again, I hopped off my bed, tore off my soaking sheets and rolled them up into a ball. I tossed them at the end of my bed and proceeded to get ready for my day.

The school year was coming to an end so graduation and college was the topic of conversation for everyone at school. I have been accepted to a couple of colleges and I narrowed my future down to one. It meant that I was going to have to move a few hours away from home and I was mentally preparing myself for dorm room living without my younger siblings or my parents. I decided to take a course in graphic design. It was very much unlike me to take a course in this field but, out of all the different possibilities, this was the one that I wanted to do more than anything.

As the chatter continued in every hall and in every classroom in regards to the upcoming graduation, one word grabbed my attention and it was then that I realized I hadn't put any thought into it... Prom!

"How could I have forgotten about prom?"

I cried to Emily. She just shrugged her shoulders.

"I just don't get why you didn't notice any of the posters!" she laughed.

I looked around and of course the walls were covered in prom posters and flyers.

"Unreal," I muttered as Emily continued to laugh at my reaction to the posters. I continued to walk to class with Emily giggling behind me.

*****

"I bought the tickets!" Jack exclaimed when he saw me at break.

"What tickets?" I asked.

He hadn't mentioned anything about needing tickets. I racked my brain in the couple of seconds before he replied, "Prom." Emily cracked up laughing again at my failed attempt to remember the most important dance of high school. I shook my head.

"You didn't ask me to prom," I teased.

"Well, Miss Trudent, if I may," Jack said as he twirled me around by my hand. "Will you do me the honour of escorting me to prom?" he asked with a beautiful smile on his face. How could I say no?

*****

After school, I went straight to my room. There was no sense in sitting downstairs with my family.

The whole episode with the kitchen was still too much for my mother. I sat down on my computer chair in front of my desk and I stared at the small pile of college letters. Some were acceptances, some were explaining why I was on the waiting list, and there was one refusal. I decided to pick up the one for graphic design. I had made my decision; I'm going to move five hours away from home and take this course for two years. I turned my chair around to get up and make my way downstairs to announce my decision when I froze in place. To my amazement, I found my dresser pushed up against my closed bedroom door making it impossible to get through. I stood there staring for a second before I put my papers down and attempted to move my dresser back to its place. I pushed and pushed and it just wouldn't budge. I tried to wedge myself in between the dresser and the wall, but there wasn't enough room. I gave up and sat on the floor. I was out of breath and moist with sweat.

"What is it now, Arnold?" I shouted. I stood up and tried once more to move the dresser, but it wouldn't budge.

"Mom!" I yelled. I hopped up onto the dresser and banged on the door and shouted, "Mom!" once more. I listened; she wasn't coming.

I jumped back down and went to the window to see if she was outside. She wasn't there. I opened the window and looked at my options. I could step up onto the ledge and shimmy down the small roof that covered the porch, then hang off the side and stand on the railing and jump down. That seemed like a good option. That actually seemed to be my only option.

I grabbed onto the window ledge, rested my right foot on the sill and I pulled my left foot up. I sat crouched down for a minute on the window ledge trying to get enough courage to step onto the roof. Just as I was ready to step down, I felt two cold hands push me out of the window. I screamed and managed to turn my body onto my stomach to grab the edge of the roof, but it was too late. I couldn't grab the edge and I fell onto the grass on my front yard. I stopped screaming when I hit the grass. I laid on the hard ground underneath the not so fluffy grass and stared up at the clouds. I felt the pain after just a second of lying there. It started at my foot and shot up my leg.

My mother came rushing out of the house and stood above me. She stared with her mouth open like she wanted to scream but nothing came out. She looked up and stared at my bedroom window with hate burning in her eyes. She then looked away from the window and gazed down at me; her eyes changed from hate to love in a split second. She bent down, sat on her knees and placed her two hands on either side of my face.

"Where does it hurt, honey?" she asked.

"My leg!" I yelled. I didn't mean to yell but it hurt so badly. I tried to sit up but my mother kept pushing me back down.

"Just stay put," she said as she stared at my window.

"What are you looking at Mom?" I asked through the breaths I was trying hard to take, hoping she was seeing Arnold.

"I'm looking at how far down you fell. What on earth were you doing?" she asked.

"I called your name and I banged on my door but you didn't hear me," I accused. She stared at my face with a look almost made of guilt. I would have thought it was guilt, had I not known any better.

"I didn't, honey. How strange," she replied.

I managed to sit up to examine the rest of my body. Now that I was sitting, breathing came easier. I had a couple of scratches on my elbows and a few on my lower back but nothing serious. A few of the neighbors came out to see what was going on, so I politely asked my mother to help me inside. We managed to get into the house, but I couldn't put any weight on my foot at all.

My mother called my father to come home from work. He was nearly done anyway so he left work so that he could take me to the hospital. I sat in the recliner while I waited for my father to come home. My foot and my leg were throbbing. My mother was sitting on the floor beside me as she applied ice to my ankle.

"Why weren't you able to use your door, Tina? What would make you jump out of the window?" she asked.

"My dresser is in front of my bedroom door and I couldn't move it. I tried but it wouldn't budge. So I banged on the door and yelled your name. When you didn't answer, I tried to climb out of the window, but it felt like someone pushed me out," I told her. She watched my face throughout my entire explanation and then shook her head.

"When the doctor examines you, have him check to see if you may have hit your head," she said as a matter of fact.

"Excuse me?" I exclaimed.

"Tina, I am so tired of these crazy stories. Maybe with graduation coming up, you're not getting enough sleep but you have to stop with these stories. You're going to tell the wrong person one day and they'll have you admitted to the psych ward!" she shouted.

"I'm not making this up. I wouldn't jump out of a window! Why won't you believe me?" I cried.

My mother shook her head and walked into the kitchen. Just then my father arrived. He came to me and kissed me on my forehead.

"Are you ready?" he asked with sympathy pain written all over his face.

"Yes!" I said. My father helped me up and into his car. I didn't say "bye" to my mother.

"What did you do?" he asked as we started on our way to the emergency.

"I fell out the window. I was trying to see if Mom was outside and I lost my balance," I lied.

106

What was the point in telling the truth? He looked at me questioningly but didn't persist.

The hospital was only five minutes away but the wait was nearly three hours. I sat in a wheelchair with my leg high up; I felt silly but my leg felt better being up high. After a half hour of waiting, my father went home to pick up my iPod and a book to keep me busy.

While he was gone, only one person was called in but three other patients arrived at the emergency room. One person was a male, around fifty five-sixty years old. He looked like he was having a hard time breathing and I heard him say something about chest pains to the triage nurse, so they brought him in immediately. The second person was a child and his mother; he looked to be about nine years old. It looked like he got glass or something in his foot. With all that blood, I was sure stitches were going to be needed. They sat across from me; the mother smiled at me so I smiled back. The third person to arrive was a teenage girl with no noticeable injury. She, too, sat across from me but didn't look up long enough to even make eye contact with anyone.

When my father came back, he was full of questions.

"Why in the world was your dresser in front of your door?" he asked. "I asked your mother to run up to get your things and she had to call me up to open the door! I had to push the dresser away with the door, squeeze my way through the door and the wall, and then push the dresser back to where it belongs!" He finished his rant and stared at me for an answer.

"I dropped something in behind it and moved it over. When I tried to move it back, I couldn't, so I called for Mom, but she didn't hear me. So, I looked out of the window for her, but she wasn't out there and that's when I fell out," I lied again. The lying was getting easier, but the frustration was very thick.

"Okay," was all my father said.

We sat in silence for a while and I played a game on my cell phone. I tried to open my book to read, but I couldn't concentrate on anything.

"Dad, do you believe me when I tell you that I am being haunted?" I whispered.

"Tina, I really don't believe in that stuff. But if you truly believe that someone from the other side is trying to hurt you, then I could listen. I will listen, with my full attention to you," he replied. It was a nice gesture, but I was tired of explaining.

"Thanks Dad," was all I could say. He didn't react to my cold response; he simply looked up and continued to watch the hockey game that was playing on the hospital TV.

*****

When we arrived home, I felt better. They wrapped my broken ankle up really tight and gave me a referral to see a specialist in the morning to get a cast put on my leg. They also gave me some pain medication that made the throbbing in my ankle almost immediately subside. It was pretty late when we got home and my mother was nowhere in sight, so I asked my father to help me up the stairs. Until I got the cast in the morning, putting pressure on my foot wasn't a good idea. Once we got to the top, I was okay to continue on my own. They gave me a crutch for support but using that to go up the stairs was kind of a death trap for me.

"I'll take the morning off tomorrow to bring you to the specialist. Have a good night, Tina," my father said and he kissed the top of my head.

"Good night, Dad," I replied. I looked around my room. My father had slid my dresser back into place but everything that was on it before was still on the floor. I attempted to bend down and reach for the bottles of lotions and perfumes, some papers and a few pens and a highlighter, but quickly decided against it and climbed into bed. *I'll get that stuff in the morning*, I thought.

*****

I slept well, right up until morning. I woke with a start just minutes before my alarm clock went off. I had my dream again, but this time it was a little different. There was someone running beside me. We were both running from Arnold, but I couldn't see who it was. Every time I looked over as we ran through the forest, they would look away; I couldn't even tell if they were a male or female. They wore a black hoodie. They ran and kept up right beside me. When I tripped over that same root that I always trip over, the person tried to grab my arm and pull me away but, as usual, it was too late.

I stayed in bed for a few minutes longer going over my dream and trying to place who that person may have been, but I couldn't see their face. I gave up trying to recognize the person and swung my leg up, forgetting that it was broken. I let out a yell but nothing to have anyone come running into my room for apparently. I managed to get up, get dressed and head to the top of the stairs. It seemed like everyone was already downstairs, so I attempted and managed to make it down the stairs holding the railing with my right hand and the crutch in my left. My family was downstairs eating breakfast and looked surprised to see me.

"Why didn't you yell for your Dad?" my mother asked.

"I was fine; I made it," I said as I grabbed a bowl and made myself a bowl of cereal. My mother watched me for a few seconds then asked how I was. "My ankle is throbbing but I just took a pain pill so I should be okay soon." I was acting cold towards her for the way that she had treated me when I told her how I broke my ankle.

"Well, try to stay off of it until your cast is

110

on," she advised. I replied with a nod.

*****

The specialist at the hospital took me in right away. I needed another x-ray but I didn't ask why. I just wanted to get my cast on and go home. I wasn't going to school that day and I didn't call Emily or Jack last night so they were probably already wondering where I was.

Everyone at the specialist's office was really nice. I got my cast on and as I walked out, without a crutch, I said, "Goodbye and thank you." And they all replied jokingly by telling me to stay away from open windows. I smiled politely and left. I know they were just being friendly but I wished someone would believe me.

*****

I spent the day in my room. I cleaned up the mess that I had attempted to clean the night before and rested in my bed for the rest of the day. My mother periodically brought me food and drinks throughout the day and she was rather pleasant. She wasn't moping anymore. I didn't bring up the fall and neither did she. She asked me about prom and I told her that Jack and I were going.

"I have an account that I opened for you when you were a baby. It's for special occasions, like this one," she said.

"Really?" I asked excitedly.

"Yes, it's mainly for school but when I opened the account I thought about your prom and decided that we'd use it for this too," she smiled. "How long is the cast on for?" she asked. I smiled.

"Six weeks! And prom is in nine weeks!" I said. I was happy that I didn't have to go to prom with a broken ankle.

"Well, when your cast is off, you and Emily can go shopping for a dress!" she said smiling.

My mother left me so that I could rest. I laid in my bed and thought about different styles and colours for my prom dress. I looked forward to my shopping trip.

When school was over, I made sure to grab my phone. I knew Emily and Jack would be calling. Sure enough, the phone rang and Emily was on the line.

"Where were you today?" she asked.

"At home. I broke my ankle yesterday after school and I had to go to the specialist this morning to get a cast put on," I explained.

"How did you break your ankle? Are you okay? Do you need me to come over? Will you be in a cast for prom?" Her questions were pouring out so fast that I had a hard time keeping up.

"I fell out of my window, yes I'm okay, you don't need to come over, I'm fine, and my cast will be off two weeks before prom," I replied with a smile. She was always so sweet.

"How does someone fall out of a window?" she asked.

"Well, it helps when a ghost pushes you out," I answered.

She was quiet. I broke the silence.

"It's okay, I'm fine and I'm going to call France for a reading. Maybe she can help figure out why he wants to hurt me," I said. She agreed.

We hung up the phone but I kept mine in my hand knowing that it wouldn't be long before Jack called. Within seconds, the phone was ringing again.

"Hello?" I answered.

"Hey! Are you okay?" he asked in a confused tone.

"Yeah, I'm fine but I spent a few hours in the hospital last night and a bit today to get a cast on my leg," I said and waited for the questions. He asked the normal "hows" and "whens" and I answered them all with the truth.

"Are you kidding me? I wish he were alive so I can kill him myself!" was his reaction. Feeling flattered, I let him go and told him that I would see him at school the following day.

I went down for supper. I still wasn't very good at walking with my cast but I was getting around. I sat at my place at the table and my mother placed my plate of food in front of me. I thanked her and dug into my spaghetti as we chatted about the weather, my father's work and anything else to avoid the silence. I didn't want to

113

talk about my leg and I'm sure my mother didn't want to talk about my ghost.

If there was anything I loved best, it was watching Heidi eat spaghetti. I looked at her and smiled as she slurped up a noodle. I looked over at Tommy whose high chair, as well as his precious little face, was covered in noodles and sauce. I made a silly face at him and waited for his smile. I got one that made noodles fall out of his mouth and onto his tray. I laughed and took another fork full of my supper.

After supper, I volunteered to do the dishes but my mother shooed me out of the kitchen. I went back upstairs and into my room to call France. I wanted to make an appointment for a reading.

"Okay, thank you! I will see you in two days!" I replied as I hung up with her. Getting an appointment with her that soon was pure luck! I looked forward to Thursday night.

*****

I took the city bus to school the next morning. Emily and Jack waited for me at the bus stop. I got double the hugs that morning; they made me laugh.

"C'mon you guys! I'm fine," I told them.

"You were pushed out of a damn window!" Jack exclaimed.

"Yeah and you two are the only ones who believe me, so let's not make a big deal about it. I will heal and this will be forgotten," I said as a matter of fact.

They both shook their heads as we started to walk towards the school. As we got closer, I noticed all the looks and stares of students who were curious about my leg.

"Let's just go straight inside," I said as I nodded and smiled to a few friends.

"Yep," replied Jack as Emily followed.

I made it through the day with a few questions. My lie on "falling" out of the window was believable and students and teachers accepted it.

Jack wanted to take me out for supper that night. He had it all planned out and even borrowed his mother's car that morning. I called my mother from school to let her know my new plans. There was no answer so I left a voicemail telling her that I would be home no later than seven pm.

When the final bell rang, I got up from my desk and gathered all my things. I bent down to pick up my school bag when I felt Jack's warm embrace from behind me. I closed my eyes and inhaled his delicious cologne.

"Thought you could use a hand," he said as he came around to the front of me and quickly kissed my cheek in the process. I smiled.

"I'm fine, really," I promised. But he gathered up my things for me and placed them in my school bag.

When he was done, he flung my school bag over his shoulder beside his and took my hand. He made jokes to the people we knew in the hallways about him needing to do everything for me now. I just followed and shook my head with a smile. He led me to his mother's red sports car and helped me in. I rolled my eyes but accepted his help.

Jack took me to a small restaurant that served homemade dishes. It was my favourite restaurant. I ordered the lasagna with garlic bread and a Caesar salad; Jack ordered the same. It was delicious. We talked about everything but my home situation. I was too tired to even think about the Trepherd family that haunted my house.

We were too stuffed to eat dessert but it came with our meals so I took the chocolate cake to go and Jack ordered the apple pie. I thanked him again for supper and we headed to my place.

"My pleasure," he said.

"I'm sorry for wanting to go home so early but I'm still new with this cast and it makes me tired," I apologized.

"It's okay, I understand. I just can't wait for it to come off," he said and he kissed my hand but kept his eyes on the road.

When we turned onto my road, we noticed a couple of police cars.

"Are they at my place?" I asked Jack as I squinted to see better. We were still a little too far to be sure.

"I think so..." he replied but he too was

116

staring hard to see for sure.

As we got closer, we saw three police cars; two in front of my house and one blocking my driveway. I panicked.

"What do you think happened?" I asked Jack as I rushed out of the car. He didn't answer. He rushed around the car to help me get to the front door.

When we went in, we made our way through two police officers who didn't give us a hard time. One officer asked who we were and Jack told them that I lived there. I found my mother sitting on the couch crying and my father standing beside her. He looked bewildered.

"What happened?" I asked. My father looked up but couldn't speak. Every time he tried to, his bottom lip and chin would quiver.

"Mom! What's going on?" I shouted.

She looked up at me and said, "Heidi."

"Heidi what, Mom? What's wrong with Heidi?" I demanded. An officer came up behind me.

"Heidi went missing this afternoon. From your mother's statement, it looks like it was around two pm this afternoon," he answered.

I went numb and my knees gave out. Jack caught me before I fell to the floor. It took a second before I could stand on my own. Jack helped me to the lazy boy and went to the kitchen to get me a glass of water. I thanked him and took a quick sip. When I was able to think straight, I started to remember different hiding spots that Heidi liked to use.

"Did you check everywhere?" I asked nobody in particular.

"Yes, honey, I looked everywhere and so did your Dad; she's not here," my mother said and started to cry into a tissue that was balled up in her hands.

My father sat next to her and hugged her. He didn't cry; he chose a spot on the floor and stared at it. Tommy was in his chair holding a toy but he was looking around at everyone instead of playing with it. I bent down so I could reach his tiny head and I kissed it. He kicked his feet as he squealed in delight.

"You're being so good," I said to him in a low voice. "I'll be back to play with you," I told him as he smiled his beautiful smile.

Jack and I went upstairs. The police were gathering up their things including a picture of my precious sister and they were getting ready to leave. I heard them tell my parents to call them if they heard anything.

I went into Heidi's room and looked around. Nothing looked out of the ordinary. I looked under her bed and in the closet; I don't know if I expected to find her but I was still disappointed that she wasn't there. I went into all the rooms and did the same thing. No sign of Heidi.

"Jack, do you think we could drive around

for a bit? I can't sit in this house without her," I said. I didn't cry, I held myself together, but my hands wouldn't stop shaking. I accepted all the help that Jack gave me.

We drove around the blocks that surrounded my house for three hours. I had my head out the window the whole time and searched for my little sister but there was no sign of her. Finally, I gave up and Jack took me back home. Before we got out of the car, I took his hand and thanked him for helping me try to find her.

"Jack, I'm going to go up to my room and lie down for a bit. I will call you later. Okay?" I asked. All of a sudden, I was emotionally drained.

"Of course. Call me if you hear anything," he said. He kissed me on my forehead and got out of the car to help me back inside and up to my room. He left quietly. I could hear Jack saying goodbye to my parents.

I laid down on my bed and I started to cry, I couldn't stop. I could feel my eyelids swell as the tears kept coming. I asked myself where she could have gone, how she could have left without my mother seeing her, and who could have taken her.

I heard Heidi's laugh; it sounded so sweet.

"Over here," she shouted when I lost sight of her. She was running in a beautiful field. I laughed and ran to her. I didn't have my cast on and I felt free. She was so beautiful with the sun shining in her hair making her blonde strands glow.

I reached out to hug her but she was gone; she disappeared right before my eyes. I looked around and it grew dark. I was in my house. I tried a light switch and nothing happened.

"Heidi!" I yelled. "Where did you go?" I searched every room in my house but she was gone. I started to cry again; big heavy sobs were coming from my chest and out of my mouth. I looked down and my cast was back. I started limping through the hallway, shouting once again for my sister.

"Tina! I'm here, I'm playing hide and seek! Come find me!" I heard her sweet voice call out and her beautiful laugh trail behind her. I started awkwardly running towards her voice but I couldn't catch up to her.

"Heidi, slow down; where are you?" I called out.

"I'm hiding!" she yelled back with a giggle. It came from the room I was standing in front of. I stepped back to make out what room it was. It was Heidi's.

I woke up and I sat straight up. I looked at my clock, 2:42 am. I jumped out of bed and ran as fast as my leg would let me to Heidi's room. I opened the door and switched on the light. I looked around. My gut was telling me not to give up.

"Heidi!" I shouted. I heard her giggle!

"Heidi, where are you?" I asked as I walked

towards her closet.

"It's a game, Tina; I can't tell you!" she said with a laugh.

I opened the closet door and there she was.

"You found me! But you cheated; you're not s'pose to ask where I am!" she sulked. I dropped to my knees and hugged my little sister and covered her face with kisses.

"Mom! Dad!" I yelled as loudly as I could. They were still downstairs. I heard them run upstairs; one of them tripped but quickly got up and kept going.

They ran to Heidi's room where I was still on my knees hugging her. I looked up and they both started crying and called her over to them. She looked confused and went to them.

"I was just playing, I'm sorry," Heidi said and started to cry as my parents hugged her.

"Where was she?" my mother asked me as she wiped the tears that were still flowing from her eyes.

"In her closet, she said she was playing hide and seek," I told them.

"How did you know to come in here?" my mother asked.

"I had a feeling," I replied. I didn't tell her about the dream.

"You must be tired?" she asked Heidi.

"No, I'm hungry," she replied. We all laughed and went down to eat. Heidi wanted grilled cheese and my mother was happy to make it.

While my mother cooked, my father called the police. The police had a few questions so they came by. My parents didn't mind as we were all awake except Tommy, but he slept through anything.

When Officer David and Officer Sam arrived, they sat on the love seat across from where Heidi was sitting. They both smiled at her.

"What were you doing all day?" Officer David asked Heidi.

"Playing hide and seek mostly," replied Heidi.

"Well, that sounds like fun! Where were all the places that you hid?" he asked.

"Mostly in the closets," she said with her mouth full of cheesy toasted bread.

My mother, father and I all sat around and listened to the answers that Heidi gave the officer. We all couldn't help but smile at her answers; we missed her so much.

"Did you hear your Mom and Dad calling your name? They were looking for you all day," he asked her still smiling.

"Yes, but I thought they were playing too," she said. She brought her eyes down as though she was being punished.

"That was a long game," Officer Sam said with a laugh. That made Heidi smile again as she nodded.

"Who were you playing hide and seek with Heidi?" he asked as she took a gulp of milk.

"Arnold," she replied without looking up. I looked up from my plate at my little sister.

My blood ran cold and my hands turned to ice. I could feel my heart pumping harder to move the blood through my body. My head was spinning. I heard the officer ask another question but I couldn't make out the question nor her answer. I breathed through my nose and out my mouth. When I was able to see and think straight, I looked at my parents. They didn't seem fazed. They just sat and smiled at Heidi and the officers.

"She also has an imaginary friend named Holly," my mother told Officer David.

It was then that I excused myself and went back up to my room. I wanted to scream but I didn't. I went to bed hoping that my reading with France would give me some answers.

Chapter 6

I didn't sleep that night. I tossed and turned while thoughts played in my head. What did Arnold want with my sister? What kind of point was he trying to make? Why were my parents so oblivious to the haunting that was happening in this house?

I laid in my bed, thought about all these questions and I heard everything that was going on downstairs. I heard my parents come up to bed and tuck Heidi in. I heard them check on me but I pretended that I was already asleep.

My alarm clock went off. It was pointless to let it go off, since I was awake, but I kept my head on my pillow and stared at my alarm clock until it buzzed. I turned it off but stayed in my bed for a few more minutes. I had thoughts of not going to school that day but being so close to graduation, I didn't want to take any chances.

*****

Jack followed me around all day at school again. He helped me with all my books and carried my school bag. I was mentally preparing myself for my visit with France so I was in a daze during my classes and with my friends. Everyone wrote it off due to the fact that I had a cast and it was still new. I smiled and nodded and continued my daydreams about getting some answers.

*****

I took the city bus to France's house. The bus stop was only five houses away from hers. I stepped off the bus and made my way to 112 Altoy Rd. I jumped when she opened the door before I had a chance to knock. I smiled to myself, guessing she knew I was here, and I followed her into her home. She had a beautiful place. The walls were all painted in neutral colours and her furniture was all modern. I really wasn't expecting this. France was in her fifties; she was single and very pretty. She dressed in a hippy style fashion which is probably the reason for my shock at her decorating choices.

She led me to a table in a small room off of the kitchen. I sat across from her. I was expecting a glass ball and I asked her about it. She laughed.

"Is this your first time?" she asked.

"Aside from the time that you came to my place, yes," I answered. She nodded and she pulled out some cards. She started flipping the cards and had an explanation for each one that was flipped. I listened attentively but this wasn't what I wanted to know; I wanted to know why I was being harassed by a ghost. She told me things like "I have an old soul." But I needed to know more.

"You have a spirit in your house who doesn't leave you alone. He has a wife and a daughter too that you have come in to contact with?" she asked. *Finally*, I thought.

"Yes! What does he want?" I asked. She put her hand up to show me to be patient.

"He has a connection with you. You meant something to him in your past life," she said. "He is angry with you for moving on and having a new life." France talked with her eyes closed. I couldn't help but stare at her as she spoke. "He won't stop until you..." she stopped and squinted as though she was trying to understand the demand.

"Until I what?" I demanded. My fists hit the top of her table. I realized what I had done so I slipped my hands under the table onto my lap and waited for her to finish.

"Until you right the wrong," she finished.

"Until I right the wrong? What wrong?" I asked. She shook her head.

"I'm sorry, that's all I got, she says no more," she replied. She started to clean up. I stared at her in disbelief.

"She? Do you mean Amelia? Amelia spoke to you?" I asked.

"Yes, it was a woman that was talking to me." She continued to clean up the table. She got up and motioned for me to do the same. I did and she led me to the door.

"There is nothing I can do to make him leave. You either have to deal with him or figure out the wrong that happened in your past life, but he's not going anywhere," she said. I shook my

126

head and paid her for her services.

I walked to the bus stop and sat on the bench. I repeated the words "right the wrong" in my head. Those words didn't make sense to me; I didn't know how this could be possible.

I arrived at my house just in time for dinner.

*****

I woke up in the middle of the night to the sound of my mother crying. She wasn't crying loud but I heard her. I slowly got out of bed, tiptoed across the hall and peered into her and my father's room. There she was lying on her stomach with her head turned facing the doorway that I was in. Her eyes were open but she didn't see me; she was focusing on something or someone.

"Arnold," I heard my mother whisper through her tears. I looked over and my father was fast asleep. She laid there for a few more minutes crying silently when, all of a sudden, she took a breath. She sat up and took several more breaths and hugged her knees to her chest. I didn't go to her. I hid behind the door jamb and watched.

"Ron, wake up!" she shouted as she shook my father awake. He sat up stunned at his rude awakening.

"What is it?" he questioned as he rubbed his eyes.

"I think I had a nightmare!" she cried. "I

was just lying in bed but I couldn't move. I felt paralyzed," my mother said as she wiped her tears away.

"What happened?" my father asked.

"I can't remember but it was bad; I have the worst feeling!" she panicked as she spoke. She stopped and took some deep breaths. I walked away. I felt mean and cold not going to see if she was okay, but I guess if she was going to ever believe me, this would have to be the way. I was also afraid that my mother still wouldn't believe me. I climbed back into my bed and spent the night dreaming about being chased in the forest and always waking up when Arnold's hands reach down to grab me.

*****

"It's a good movie!" Emily said when I was hesitant on the movie she chose. It was about a serial killer who cut off people's heads.

"It's a little too much for me," I said as I looked at other movie titles.

"C'mon! You'll be fine!" she coaxed. I sighed and gave in. I followed her to the box office.

"I'm gonna regret this!" I said as we headed into the theatre room to find some seats. I cringed and screamed throughout the entire movie and I hated every second of it. I looked over at Emily from time to time and her smile couldn't be any bigger.

When the movie was finished, we got in line to exit the theatre. It was packed. *I don't know how so many people could want to see this movie*, I thought to myself. When we finally exited the building, I caught sight of the most beautiful smile.

"Jack!" I exclaimed. "I thought you left to go fishing with your Dad all weekend?" I asked.

"He decided against going since the weather isn't going to cooperate and it will be too cold," he said with a smile as he kissed me on my forehead.

"Glad you didn't go! Emily probably had plans to torture me all weekend! She already had me watch a horrible movie!" I teased. Emily shook her head.

"Baby," she said under her breath as she smiled.

Jack wrapped his arms around me tightly.

"I guess I have to treat you to a better movie tomorrow night," he promised.

We all walked back to my place with smiles as we laughed and joked together.

The weekend was great! Jack took me to see a romantic movie Saturday night just as he promised. Emily refused to come with us claiming that she felt like a third wheel.

"Stop that!" I begged. "You're my best friend; you're part of my wheel!" I said. She laughed and told me to have fun.

*****

"My Mom wants to take us dress shopping for prom tonight!" I told Emily on Wednesday morning.

"Oh good! I'm excited. I know just the style and colour that I want!" she said. Emily has been saving up for prom for over a year.

"Of course you do," I said and I rolled my eyes. She giggled. She knew I was jealous of her organizational skills.

"You don't know what you want?" she asked me. I shook my head. I had no idea.

Joel had asked Emily to prom.

"I don't know why you and Joel don't make your relationship official; you do everything together," I asked. She shrugged her shoulders and pushed about my prom dress.

"I think you should go with a blue dress to match your eyes," she suggested. I agreed.

Emily ate over at my house; we had chicken finger wraps. I made mine with a whole bunch of vegetables and a lot of hot sauce. Emily simply made a Caesar salad and poured it on top of her chicken fingers and folded her wrap.

"Thanks for dinner!" Emily said to my mother just as she dried the last plate and put it away. I washed the dishes and my mother cleaned off the table and swept the floor.

"You're very welcome Emily, anytime," she replied. "Are you ladies ready to shop?" my mother asked with a smile.

I threw my wet dishcloth into the sink and Emily hung her drying towel on the rack and we were ready in seconds.

"You ladies seem excited," my mother teased.

Emily and I giggled and headed to the car. I got in the front seat with my mother and Emily got in the back. We turned the music up really loud and the three of us sang along to the radio the whole way to the store.

When we got to the boutique, we were in awe. The minute the front doors opened, all we saw were beautiful wedding and bridesmaids dresses, mother of the bride dresses and of course prom dresses. Everything was beautiful. Emily and I browsed through the gowns and eventually branched off into different sections of the store. Every now and then, we'd find each other and ask what we thought of the picks that we had draped over our arms. My mother was choosing different dresses and asking our opinions on her choices for us.

Three hours later, we were both settled on our dresses. Emily chose a burgundy classic strapless sweetheart evening gown. I chose a long V-neck sequin formal dress in baby blue. Emily and I were both proud of our choices but were both saddened that we had to leave our dresses there for the next four weeks for the alterations. I gave my dress a final glance and left the store.

"Thank you so much, Mom! I love my

dress!" I shouted over the music in the car on the way home.

"Me too!! Thank you so much for taking me with you!" Emily yelled. My mother laughed at our enthusiasm.

"You are both so welcome! I look forward to seeing you both in them," she replied.

My mother dropped Emily off at her place and then we headed home. I thanked my mother once more before heading up to my room for the night.

*****

I ran with all my might through the forest. I kept looking back.

"Arnold! Why?" I shouted as I ran.

He threw me an evil smile and kept up to me. I tried using every muscle in my body to run faster than him but he was always right behind me. I looked to my left; a child was running right beside me. I looked down and I had the child by the hand and my grip was tight. The child had a hoodie on and it was blocking its face.

"What does he want?" I asked. I watched as the hooded face turned towards me. I didn't recognize the face but I knew exactly who this child was.

Still running and still holding hands, the child continued to keep up. I looked back once more at Arnold, who was almost within arm's reach of me, and that's when I tripped over a tree root. The child stopped and stared at me before she tugged on my arm to get up and continue to run.

"Run Holly!" I shouted.

I woke up in a cold sweat and sat up.

"Holly," I whispered. I sat on my bed for a few seconds before I hopped out and wobbled over to my closet to grab another sheet. As I changed the sheet on my bed, I played with the puzzle pieces from my dreams.

When my clean sheet was on, I climbed back into bed. I thought a little more about my dream but I couldn't put the puzzle pieces together; I needed more. I tried to fall back to sleep in hopes that I would dream that dream again to maybe get more answers. Maybe this was the key to righting the wrong.

*****

"Good morning, birthday girl!" I shouted to Heidi from the stairway. I didn't see her but I knew she was downstairs.

"Tina! Look!" she yelled back excitedly. I rounded the corner and to my surprise there sat my little sister with a tiny puppy on her lap. I got down on my knees in front of Heidi and smiled.

"Happy birthday, sweetie," I said and kissed her on the forehead.

"Can I hold your puppy?" I asked.

"Yes," she answered. I scooped her little

puppy up into my hands. She was an eight week old white and tan shih tzu.

"Who got you a puppy?" I asked as the puppy licked my nose.

"Mommy and Daddy did!" she answered and squealed with delight. I laughed.

"What's your puppy's name?" I asked her as I handed the puppy back to her.

"Skittles!" she replied.

"Cute!" I said and walked into the kitchen.

"You bought Heidi a puppy?" I asked my mother when I sat down at the kitchen table.

My mother was making her special birthday breakfast this morning. Every year, we all get this amazing breakfast for our birthdays. It consists of eggs, bacon, toast, home fries and pancakes.

"Yes, I know it's more work for me but we were talking about getting a dog anyway so this was our perfect opportunity," she replied. I nodded.

"She's cute," was all I said in return. I wasn't angry but I may have been a bit jealous. I always asked for a puppy but never got one because my parents were never ready for one.

*****

When I arrived home from school, the puppy was barking and crying. I put my school bag down and went to the kitchen to see what the commotion was all about. Skittles was sitting in the corner all by herself barking and crying at nothing. I went over to her and picked her up. She cuddled into my neck and fell asleep.

"Were you lonely?" I asked her as I sat on the couch with her and let her sleep. I never owned a dog so this was a new experience for me. I pulled my casted leg up onto the couch and got comfortable so I moved her onto my lap and we both fell asleep for a bit.

When I woke up, my mother and Heidi were just coming in. Heidi came running for me as soon as she saw Skittles in my lap. I laughed and handed the puppy to her. I got off the couch and went up to my room to wrap up Heidi's birthday present. I used two weeks of my allowance to buy her a big crayon case and a couple of colouring books. When I was done, I put them in a gift bag and made my way back downstairs.

"Happy third Birthday!" I shouted. Heidi stood up and started hopping up and down in excitement. The poor puppy rolled off her legs and onto the floor, but she shook it off and ran to a slipper that was sitting beside the couch.

Heidi took my present and ripped it open; I couldn't help but laugh. She was so excited.

We went out for supper for Heidi's birthday; another birthday tradition. We always go out to the restaurant of the birthday person's choice. Heidi chose a chicken restaurant. They served amazing chicken.

"Good choice!" I told Heidi in between bites. She sat up straight with a proud look on her little face.

When the waitress came to take our dessert orders, I picked up my menu. She started with my parents. As I looked through all of the yummy choices, I felt like I was being stared at, so I looked up and spotted a family at the table just across from where I was sitting. I dropped my menu and stared back. There sat Arnold, Amelia and Holly. Arnold laughed at my reaction but didn't take his eyes off of me. The waitress made her way to me, blocking sight of the Trepherd family. I rudely ignored the waitress and moved my body to get a view of the table behind her.

"Tina!" my mother barked. I jumped at her voice but stood up to get a better view. The table was empty and completely cleaned and setup for the next customers. I sat back down and looked at my mother. She was staring at me in disbelief with her hand out at her sides.

"Sorry," I said. I looked at the waitress; she had a small smile on her face. "I don't want dessert, but thank you," I said to her.

"It comes with your meal, sweetheart. Take your time," she said to me.

"Thank you. I'll have the chocolate mousse cake," I answered. The minute she walked away, my mother turned to me.

"What was that about?" she practically shouted.

"Sorry, I thought I saw something."

"You okay, Tina?" Heidi asked me.

136

"Of course I am! Are you having a good birthday?" I asked her to change the subject.

"It's the bestest!" she replied. We all laughed. When the waitress came back with our desserts, I ate mine and I was not disappointed.

*****

I woke up to the sound of Skittles barking again. She was downstairs and it was 6:00 am.

"Does anybody else hear her?" I shouted. Nobody replied. I practically fell trying to get out of my bed. "I can't wait for this cast to come off," I mumbled to myself.

I made it down the stairs without breaking my neck. Skittles was in the kitchen and in the same corner that I had found her in the last time. I went to her, picked her up and brought her upstairs with me. I knew that she was sleeping in Heidi's room that night but I couldn't figure out how she made it out of her room and down the stairs. I checked in on Heidi; her door was opened enough for the puppy to get out and she was still fast asleep. Still holding Skittles, I checked my parent's room and they were both still sleeping. I found it odd that I was the only one who heard the poor puppy. I went back to my room and closed the door. Skittles was lucky that she didn't hurt herself in the stairs. I set her down on my bed and she walked over to my pillow and made herself comfortable. I smiled and climbed in beside her. I didn't want to disturb her and I didn't want her to fall off of my bed, so I picked up my pillow and placed it against the wall. I grabbed one of my throw pillows and used that for my head and fell back to sleep.

"You're lucky you're cute," I whispered.

*****

I woke up to my little sister screaming.

"Where is Skittles?" she yelled in the hallway. I sat up and looked around but Skittles wasn't with me anymore.

I frantically looked under the blankets and under my pillows but she wasn't there. I hopped off of my bed and checked underneath but there was only a magazine that must have fallen through the crack. I started to panic because I knew that I was the last person she was with.

I opened my bedroom door and something on my dresser caught my eye. Skittles' collar! I picked it up and stared at it as I rubbed my thumb across it. My mother burst into my already opened bedroom door and was about to say something when she noticed the collar.

"Why do you have the puppy's collar?" she asked with her eyes glued to the collar.

"I'm not sure; it was on my dresser," I replied. My mother's eyes turned cold and she snatched the collar out of my hands.

"Where is Skittles?" she demanded through clenched teeth.

"Mom, I don't know," I told her. "But she was in here last night. I woke up at six this morning to her barking so I put her in bed with me. When I woke up, she was gone," I said as I opened up my closet in hopes that she might be in there.

"You're lying!" my mother accused. "You were jealous of Heidi for having a puppy. I saw it in your face yesterday morning when you asked me about her. I felt bad and was thinking about getting you one too but then you pull this!" she shouted.

"Mom! You sound like a crazy person! What's going on? What do you think I did with the puppy?" I asked her.

"You tell me! Did you give it away? Maybe to your friend?" she accused. She was being unreasonable.

"Okay Mom, enough!" I shouted back. "I love Heidi and I love that little puppy! I wouldn't hurt Heidi like that even if I was jealous and I cannot believe that you have it in you to accuse me of doing something so horrible!" I cried. I wiped a tear from my cheek. My mother stared at me as she took in what I had just said. Then, she looked down at the collar that she held in her hand.

"I'm sorry Tina, but I don't believe you," she said and walked out of my room.

I stood there in disbelief for a minute but I started to cry. I cried for the mother who once believed in me and listened to the things that I believed in. I sat on my bed for a moment to catch my breath and then I got up again to look for

Skittles. I looked in all of my drawers and in my hamper. I looked under my desk and near my shoes but she wasn't in my room.

I got dressed and I went downstairs. I grabbed my school bag and kissed Heidi, who was still crying uncontrollably, and I promised to help her look for Skittles when I got home. I kissed Tommy on the top of his head and I left my house without even looking at my mother.

*****

"So they got Heidi a puppy?" Emily asked. "Isn't she kind of young?" she asked before I had a chance to say anything else.

"Yes, I thought that it was strange but she said that she wanted a dog for the house and used it as a birthday gift for Heidi," I explained. "I always wanted a puppy but I never got one," I complained. Emily nudged my shoulder with a laugh and called me a "cry baby." I laughed even though I was telling the truth.

"Where do you think the puppy went?" she asked.

"I don't know. Maybe there is a vent that the puppy was able to get into?" I said. "Maybe she's roaming the house from the inside of the walls." I laughed at the idea but decided that I would check when I got home that afternoon.

"My Mom has been acting strange with me ever since I started telling her about Arnold and his

140

family. Oh! I didn't tell you but I saw her crying in her sleep the other night and she said his name," I told Emily.

"Whose name?" she asked.

"Arnold," I replied. She gasped.

"Really? Does she remember?" she asked.

"I'm not sure. She never mentioned anything and didn't mention it to my Dad when she woke up," I said.

We quietly made out way to first class together, neither one of us had much more to say.

*****

It's been two weeks since Skittles went missing and she was nowhere to be seen. I did check the vents in the walls but she wasn't there. There was actually no way of her getting in them anyways. Heidi has come to terms with it and talked about Skittles only as a memory.

My cast was to come off in two weeks and I was really excited about that. I couldn't wait to soak in the tub again.

"I'm going up to my room," I told my mother on a Saturday afternoon. Emily was shopping with her mother and Jack finally went on his fishing trip with his father. I decided to go up and take a nap.

Once I got to my room, there were things that needed to be done before I could lie down. I grabbed the pile of clothes that my mother left for me on the top of the dresser and I hung the few sweaters that were folded and a couple of pairs of pants. I opened my third drawer from the top and placed my T-shirts in it. I, then, threw my socks and underwear in the top drawer. I went to my desk and tidied up the small mess. I put the pencils and eraser in the drawer and organized all the papers. When that was done, I climbed onto my bed and closed my eyes.

I didn't realize I had fallen asleep until I looked down as I ran and my cast was gone. It didn't make a difference that I knew I was dreaming because I was still just as scared as I always was of this dream. I ran with all my might with Holly's hand wrapped tightly around mine. I looked back and Arnold was right behind us.

"Come on Holly!" I shouted as I tried to run faster.

Holly didn't say anything but I felt the determination in her little hand to run faster. I looked behind us again and something was different; Arnold was holding a gun.

"Oh no!" I yelled. "Run Holly. We need to run!" But it didn't fail; I tripped over that same tree root and woke up still as frightened as the first time when I had that nightmare.

*****

I was in the basement later that afternoon looking for some painting supplies. I was in the mood to paint. I learned a little bit about painting a few years back. I wasn't very good at it but I enjoyed it. We didn't have a finished basement; it was mostly for storage. As I dug through the boxes and bins, I could hear some scratching and scraping. I stopped what I was doing and listened. It was coming from under a stool in the far corner. I slowly walked over; my stomach filled with butterflies and I started to tremble. I hoped that it wasn't a rat or something horrible like that. I reached the stool and looked under. There was Skittles in a small cage with a bowl of water and a bowl full of food. I fell to my good knee and I started to cry.

"Why are you in here?" I said through the tears that streamed down my face.

I ducked under the stool and pulled the cage to me. I unlatched the lock and she ran to me. She looked healthy and so happy to see me. She grew quite a bit in the two weeks that she went missing. I let her kiss my nose and then I grew still and my body filled with anger. I got up and went as quickly as I could up the stairs. When I reached the top, I yelled for my mother.

"Mom!" I yelled for the second time. She came running and stopped dead in her tracks when she saw what I was holding.

"Mom! You have to believe me now! We are being haunted by a ghost. His name is Arnold and he took Skittles from Heidi!" I said so fast that I stumbled over a couple words. "She was downstairs in a cage," I said as I handed Skittles over to my mother.

"What on earth did you do?" she asked me.

Not comprehending the accusation, I answered, "I was looking for my paint supplies and I heard Skittles scratching."

"Why are you doing this Tina?" she asked. "What are you trying to prove?" she said. I shook my head in confusion.

"Mom? I just found her," I said as my eyes started to well up again and my chin started to shiver.

"You're going to great lengths to try to keep up your ghost story. How did this dog survive for two weeks? You were obviously feeding her," she said.

"There were food dishes in her cage, Mom, but I didn't feed her!" I cried.

She shook her head and walked away. I followed her and watched Heidi's eyes light up as my mother handed Skittles to her, with a huge smile on her face as though she had retrieved the puppy. I headed to the stairs to go hide up in my room, but made a last minute decision to go outside. I thought about going for a walk but then decided against it since I hated limping. I sat on my front steps for hours. My mother never came out to see me and I didn't care to talk to her anyways.

After a couple of hours of sitting there, Jack showed up. He put a smile on my face from ear to ear.

"Why are you out here?" he asked. "I tried

calling you a few times but your cell went straight to voicemail."

"Drama. It's always drama in this house. I found my sister's puppy and my Mom is convinced that I hid her for two weeks," I explained. He shook his head.

"I can't say I'm surprised anymore. Your Mom is acting so strange lately," he replied. He sat with me for a while.

We mostly sat in silence with our fingers intertwined and my head resting on his shoulder.

"Do you want to come to my place for supper?" he asked. I accepted without thinking twice. We left and I didn't say goodbye. I hoped that my mother worried about me when I didn't come home until later.

*****

"Today's the day!" I told Emily. We were finally able to go and pick up our prom dresses.

"I hope they did a good job!" she replied.

Emily took the city bus with me back to my place.

"My Mom still isn't talking to me very much," I explained to Emily.

She nodded and we rode the city bus in silence until we reached our destination. I pulled the cord when our stop came into view. I lived a block away from the bus stop. I could tell Emily already felt uncomfortable about coming to my place, but it was the only way to get our dresses.

When we arrived at my place, we went up to my room. Emily sat on the far corner of my bed so her back was placed in the corner. I laughed at her.

"The ghosts don't jump out and go "boo." I promise," I said with a giggle. She laughed uneasily but her eyes kept moving to each corner of my room over and over again.

We heard the puppy bark over the music that I had just put on. Emily's eyes lit up; she really wanted to meet her. I turned off the music and we went downstairs. Emily went straight to Heidi and Skittles, and I went into the kitchen. I figured I'd make us our own supper and eat it in my room. I hadn't eaten at the dinner table in a week, not since my mother accused me of kidnapping Skittles.

I threw together a couple of sandwiches with a side of salad on each plate. I grabbed two sodas and went into the living room. I stood in front of Emily, without looking at my mother, until Emily noticed me. When she realized that I was standing there, I made a nodding motion with my head and my eyes told her that it was time to make our way upstairs. She swiftly got up and followed me upstairs.

"That puppy is so cute!" she said.

"Yeah, I haven't touched her since I found her," I told her. "And my Mom couldn't care less. She doesn't care that I stay in my room; she doesn't care that I make my own supper and eat by myself;

and she doesn't care that she hurt my feelings," I complained. "I can't wait for September to start college," I said.

"I can imagine!" she replied. "Maybe I can ask my Mom if you can stay with us until you leave for school?" she offered.

"Thanks, but I'll be fine. I'd miss Heidi too much," I said gloomily.

We ate our sandwiches and salads and continued to listen to music in my room for a while until my mother came up and asked if we were ready to go and pick up our dresses.

"Yes, we'll be down in a second," I told my mother and I gathered up our plates. She spun on her heels and went back downstairs. Emily took the dishes from me and we met my mother downstairs.

The ride to the boutique wasn't as fun as the first time. I didn't sit in the front with my mother; I sat in the back with Emily. There was no music playing, just silence.

The saleslady came out with Emily's dress first. Emily took it into the change room and tried it on. When she came out, she looked stunning. The gown made everything special about her stand out. Her eyes popped and it complimented every curve. She had a beautiful smile on her face. She did a few swirls before going back into the change room to put her clothes back on. They were just coming out with mine, so I stood up. I couldn't wait to try it on.

"We have an issue with your dress, Tina,"

the first saleslady said.

"Oh? What is it?" I asked. I looked at Emily with my eyebrows drawn up; she returned a confused look with a shrug of her shoulders.

When I turned back to the saleslady, she held out my dress. I drew in my breath and took a second to release it. It was torn multiple times down the front; it had black stains the entire length of the tears. It was completely ruined.

"Who would do this?" I shouted. I looked over at my mother who was standing behind me, staring at my dress; she was speechless.

"Mom!" I shouted. "What happened?" I asked her as if she had the answer.

"Do we have time to choose another dress or reorder this one with her measurements?" she asked the saleslady instead of responding to me.

"No, I'm sorry, there isn't enough time but since this happened on our property I will call my boss and see what can be done. I will contact you no later than tomorrow before 9 pm," she said.

I had no more tears to cry; I nodded my head and left the boutique. My mother stayed behind with Emily as they placed her gown in a long bag. I sat in the backseat of my mother's car and waited for them to finish.

Chapter 7

The saleslady from the boutique called the following day at 7:30 pm. My mother answered the phone and spoke with her.

"Okay, thank you. We will be right over," she said and hung up the phone.

"They found another dress for you, dear, similar to the one you had chosen, but we have to go now to try it on in order for them to have it ready in time," she said while she gathered up her purse and keys.

I stood up and went to put my shoe on my good foot and met her in the car. We drove to the boutique in silence. I was not excited about my dress and that made it hard to be excited for prom.

The saleslady was waiting for us. She pulled out the dress as soon as she saw me. It was the right colour, baby blue, but not at all the same style. This one was a high low gown so it was long in the back and shorter in the front. I tried it on and it fit perfectly. I came out so they could check if alterations needed to be made. She wanted to alter along the bottom but I told her not to bother, that it was fine. I went back into the change room and put my clothes back on.

Because of all the mix up, they gave my mother thirty percent off the dress. My mother looked at me with a smile to show me that we received a good deal. I rolled my eyes at her and walked out of the boutique and got into the car and waited.

My mother didn't say anything to me when she slipped the dress into the backseat and came around to the driver's seat. We just drove home.

*****

"I bet it's beautiful!" Jack said to me. I knew he was just trying to make me feel better.

"It's not ugly but it's not the one that I had chosen," I complained. Emily didn't say anything. She knew that my dress had been sabotaged and agreed one hundred percent with me.

"I booked an appointment with a hairdresser for us, Tina. We are both at the same time," she said with a smile. I smiled back at her but I didn't reply. I wasn't excited about prom anymore; I actually didn't even want to go.

*****

"Are you ready?" my father asked me when I got home from school.

"For what?" I asked. I was on my way up to my room.

"Your appointment to get your cast off is today! Did you forget? I thought you'd be excited," he exclaimed. With everything going on about prom and my dress, I forgot that I even had the cast on.

"Yes!" I said with the first smile I've worn in days.

"Oh wow, this feels good," I said as I bent my leg back and forth at the knee. We were in the car on our way back from the hospital. My father smiled at me.

"You'll be beautiful even if your dress had come from a bargain store. What happened to your dress is horrible; I get that but don't let it get you down," my father said. I smiled at him.

"Thanks Dad, it's just the last couple of months have been really rough and prom was going to be my escape for a night. I know that I'll still have fun but I spent three hours choosing my perfect gown," I said as a couple of tears fell onto my cheeks. My father put his arm around me.

"You'll look beautiful," he promised.

When we arrived home, Heidi came running to me with her puppy trailing right behind her.

"You can walk!" she yelled as she jumped into my arms. I laughed and squeezed her tight before I went up to my room to study.

*****

I was still studying late into the night. I looked over at my clock it was 2:42 am. *I should call it a night*, I told myself. I stood up and removed my jeans; it felt amazing to be able to wear jeans again. I walked over to my dresser and grabbed a pair of PJ bottoms. As I was putting them on, I heard my mother crying. I walked over to her bedroom, crossing the hallway quietly. I peered into her room and witnessed her being pressed up against the wall of her room by an invisible force. She was struggling and was repeating the name "Arnold." My father was once again fast asleep. Within seconds of standing at her doorway, she was released and fell to the floor. I went to her.

"Are you okay, Mom?" I asked her as I helped her up.

"Of course I am, Tina. Why am I on the floor?" she asked me.

"Do you really not know why you're on the floor, Mom?" I asked her with my eyebrows creased in.

"No," she said and pushed my arm off of hers.

"I'm fine. Please go back to bed," she said as she dismissed me. I didn't say anything in return; I turned and went back to my room.

*****

I slept at Emily's for the weekend. I needed to get away. I hated being at home and Emily's house wasn't too far from mine, so if I needed to go home I could call a taxi and be home within ten minutes. It wouldn't be an issue.

"Run!" I screamed as I pulled Holly along by the hand through the dark forest. The moon was shining bright. I looked back and Arnold was close behind.

"We need to run faster, okay, Holly?" I said. She nodded her head. We ran as fast as our muscles let us.

"Ahhh!" I yelled as I tripped over a root that stuck out of the ground. Holly tugged and tugged on my arm.

"Come on, Mommy! Get up!" she screamed at me. I looked back and woke up just as Arnold reached down to grab me.

I sat up and tried to regulate my breathing.

"Are you okay?" Emily asked. "You screamed," she said.

"I'm so sorry, Emily. I didn't want to wake you. I was afraid something like this would happen if I slept over," I told her. I had made a bed on the floor for myself and placed it right beside Emily's bed. Emily had offered her bed to me last night, but I couldn't accept it.

"It's okay; I just wanted to make sure that you were okay," she said.

"I'm fine but I think I know the link between Arnold and myself in my past life," I told her. "I was his wife!"

Emily let out a breath of air and asked me how I knew.

"I have this reoccurring dream of Arnold chasing me in the forest but each time I have it something new happens, almost like I'm getting more information during each dream. This time I was running with Holly and she called me Mommy!" I explained. Emily said nothing; she just stared at me with a look of surprise.

I got up and opened her bedroom door and peered into the hallway for her parents. I needed to use the washroom but was afraid that I may have woken them and didn't want to have to explain. All clear. I went into the washroom and locked the door. I ran some cool water in the sink and splashed my face with it. I turned around to grab the towel when I heard a laugh. I jumped and a small scream escaped my lips. I looked back into the mirror, my face still dripping wet with water, and saw Arnold standing behind me wearing an ugly smirk on his face. I quickly wiped my face and ran back to Emily's room. I shut and locked the door.

"What happened?" Emily asked.

"Nothing, I'm sorry, I just spooked myself in the washroom," I told her. She nodded and asked me once more if I was okay. I reassured her that I was and she quickly fell back to sleep. I laid on my bed made of blankets until my eyes shut on their own.

"Tina! Help, I'm stuck!" I heard my little sister scream. Her voice was muffled.

"Heidi! Where are you?" I yelled as I searched my house. I looked throughout the entire downstairs and made my way up the stairs.

"Tina!" she yelled again. The yell sounded like it was coming from downstairs, but I ignored it and continued upstairs. I knew she wasn't down there.

"Heidi! I'm upstairs. Where are you?" I yelled as I started to search her room.

"In here!" I heard her but not from her room. I left and went back into the hallway and yelled her name again. "Tina! I'm scared!" she screamed. *That came from my room*, I thought. I opened my door. I didn't see her but I searched for her. I checked under my bed and under my desk. I opened my closet but there was no sign of Heidi.

"Heidi? Can you yell my name so I can find you?" I yelled.

"Tina!" she screamed. It came from my closet but I was standing in my closet. The light wouldn't turn on. I banged on the walls; the wall to my left started to crack.

I woke and sat up fast. I was still on Emily's floor.

"Emily, I have to go. Something is wrong with Heidi," I said to her while I gave her a little shake.

"What?" she asked. She sat up and rubbed her eyes.

"I'm going home; I will call a taxi. Call me when you get up," I said as I was changing out of my PJs and into my clothes.

"Okay," she said. She waved me off and rolled back into her blanket. I doubted that she would remember that conversation in the morning.

*****

When the taxi driver brought me home, all the lights in my house were on. I looked at the clock on the dashboard.

"It's 2:42 am?" I questioned out loud.

I handed the driver some money, jumped out of the car and ran to the front door. It was unlocked. I opened the door slowly and I could hear both my parents screaming and yelling for Heidi. I could also hear Heidi screaming back.

"Mom! Dad!" I yelled as I walked in. Tommy was crying upstairs. I assumed he was in his crib.

"Tina, we can't find Heidi but we can hear her," my mother shouted at me even though I was standing three feet away from her.

"I think I might know where she is," I said with my eyes down. "Come on!" I called to both my parents as I ran up the stairs and into my room.

I threw open my closet door, pulled all the clothes off of the bar and threw them on the floor. I pressed my ear against the wall on the left side and I yelled, "Heidi!"

"Tina!" she screamed back. I can hear the smile in her scream.

"Dad! You have to break the wall! You need to tear it down!" I yelled to my father.

He didn't hesitate. He told Heidi to back away from the wall and he made a hole with his fist way above the height of Heidi, so he knew he wouldn't hit her. He put his hands in the hole and pulled downwards. As the wall was coming apart, Heidi started laughing.

"You found me, Daddy!" she said as she came into view. My father lifted her out of the rubble and turned around to stare at me.

"How did you know?" he asked me. I shrugged my shoulders.

"I had a dream," was all I said. My mother left the room without looking at me and went to fetch my little brother who was still crying.

"Well, honey, I'm glad you listened to your dream and came home," he told me. He gave Heidi another kiss and took her back to her room. He kissed my forehead on the walk by.

"How did you get into the wall?" my father asked Heidi in the hallway.

"I woke up there," was my little sister's response.

*****

"It's prom night tonight!" Jack sang into the receiver on the other end. It was late afternoon and he already sounded so excited that I couldn't help but smile and laugh.

157

"So that means that I have to get ready; so we need to hang up now," I told him in between the giggles that my body was releasing without permission. He agreed to let me go on the condition that he gets every dance tonight. Who else was I going to dance with?

Emily had borrowed her mother's car and had just arrived at my place to pick me up. We were going to get our nails done at one place, our makeup at another and then our hair at yet another place. Had it been me that planned the arrangements, everything would have been done at the same place. Since I didn't plan a thing, I decided to have fun and go with it.

We got our nails done at a small nail salon that had a funky atmosphere. The walls were coloured red and there was some heavy punk music playing loudly in the background. Everyone that worked there and the customers, who were there, were all very friendly. There was a smile on both mine and Emily's faces from the time that we arrived until the time that we left. I chose some designs that resembled butterflies on the tips of my nails with some little blue rhinestones. Emily chose the basic French manicure.

When we left the nail salon, we didn't have time to stop anywhere. We were already running late for our makeup. Emily made pretty good time in her mother's car so we were only a couple of minutes late. I didn't have any special requests for my makeup so I let them do what they thought looked best. Emily, on the other hand, should have done her makeup herself. She was barking orders left and right on everything the makeup artist was trying to do. I couldn't help but laugh at her when we left.

"I guess I could have done it myself," she said as she looked at her reflection in her rearview mirror. "It looks like I did it anyway," she finished as she adjusted the mirror back into its place.

We had a little under an hour left before our hair appointment, so we stopped at an ice cream place for some milkshakes. Emily was very chatty and that was unusual.

"Joel said that he'd wear the same coloured tie as my dress, isn't that cute?" she asked. I nodded and smiled at her. "He also said he'd dance with me," she added. I looked at her questioningly.

"Aren't you going to prom together?" I asked.

"Yes," she replied.

"Well isn't that what dates do? They colour coordinate and dance together? I bet he'll get you a drink too!" I teased.

"Shut up," she replied with a laugh. "I'm just excited."

"I know; so am I," I told her. "So are you starting to crush a little harder on Joel?" I asked her in a teasing manner.

"Yeah, I think I am. Or maybe it's the whole prom thing. It's making me feel romantic." I rolled my eyes at her for not admitting her feelings.

It was time to head over to the hair salon so we both got up and picked up our empty cups to throw them away.

The atmosphere in the hair salon was a lot different than anywhere else we went that afternoon. Nobody was smiling and no one was talking; it was very uncomfortable. My name was called first but Emily wasn't called too long after me. The hairdresser asked me what I wanted so I just replied "an up-do."

The end results were amazing considering the lack of manners and professionalism this place had. I was unable to wipe the smile from my lips. She had all of my hair up but curled it before she bobby pinned it up. She left a few curly strands all around. Emily chose to leave her hair down but with a lot of curls. Every strand of her hair was silky, long and full of beautiful curls.

We went back to my place to get ready; that's where the guys had planned to meet us. I was starving but I didn't want to ruin my appetite knowing that Jack had reserved a table for four at a fancy new restaurant in town. I did run down the stairs, however, and grabbed a handful of crackers and I scarfed them down on my way back up.

When I reached the top of the stairs, Emily came out of my room looking like a princess. She was beautiful from head to toe.

"Your turn!" she said as she moved over to make room for me to go by. I smiled and walked by her. She even smelled delicious.

I struggled to get my dress on but, when it was on, I realized how beautiful it actually was. It brought out the colour of my eyes and it flattered all of my curves. I smiled as I opened the door to my room. Emily clapped her hands and let out a little squeal.

"You look amazing!" she said.

"Thank you, you do too!" I replied.

We went downstairs together. Both my parents, along with my siblings, were waiting for us at the bottom of the stairs. My mother had her camera and was taking picture after picture. My father laughed and made a comment about her being lucky that it wasn't actual film in the camera.

Just then, the doorbell rang and my stomach filled up with thousands of butterflies. Emily took me by the arm and gave me a reassuring smile.

"Come on in boys!" my mother said as she greeted Jack and Joel at the door. They both nodded and thanked my mother as they walked past her and came to the two of us.

"You look amazing!" Jack whispered in my ear when he came around to stand beside me.

"Thank you. You look pretty good yourself," I said with a teasing smile.

"Okay guys! Time for pictures!" my mother said as she clapped her hands and shooed my father and the kids away. We laughed and followed my mother's directions for the poses she wanted to take.

When we were done taking pictures and my mother finally let us leave, we walked out of my house and faced a beautiful white limousine.

"Oh my!" I gasped. "I wasn't expecting this!" I said as I looked at Jack. He smiled, took my hand and led me to the door that our chauffeur was holding open. I thanked him and climbed in. Emily and Joel were already in the limo laughing and playing with the radio. I looked out the window to see my mother, standing on our front porch, still snapping pictures.

*****

The restaurant was beautiful. The atmosphere was elegant and inviting at the same time. Jack introduced us to the maître d' and we were seated immediately. As I looked around, I noticed that there were other students having dinner here too before the prom. Every now and again, I would feel like we were being watched. When I looked up, I noticed that we were by couples in their 40s, 50s and probably 60s; all smiling at us. I'm sure they were reliving their prom nights as they watched us. I simply smiled in their direction and turned my attention back to Jack after each time I looked up.

Dinner was delicious and so was dessert. I took a chance and had a chocolate cake, with chocolate syrup dripping off the top. I succeeded in not dripping any on myself. Emily shook her head at me when I announced that I was able to enjoy my chocolate cake without ruining my dress. For once, she was jealous of me; she had a bowl of fruit to be safe.

*****

When we returned to the limo, we were all laughing and pressing the buttons that we were allowed to press and enjoying the free water and soda that were available. Jack and Joel kept making silly faces at the cars beside us knowing that they were unable to see us. I'm sure the driver was happy to let us out when we arrived to our prom.

"It's a casino theme?" I said in amazement as we walked in.

"Were you living under a rock?" Emily asked me. "It was written all over every flyer in the school halls!" she said as she laughed at my confused look.

I looked around, it was amazing! There were blackjack tables, roulette, poker, and they even had the game war at two different tables. At the far end of the hall was the dance floor. As we approached the dance floor, the music got louder; it was amazing. There was a table set out with poker chips. Everyone received a certain amount of chips to play with throughout the night.

"Do you want to get some chips?" Jack asked as I stared at the table.

"Oh, no that's okay. I never gambled before

163

but I think this is a wonderful idea!" I said.

Jack led me to the dance floor and we met up with Emily and Joel. We danced for hours, only stopping for a drink once in a while.

By the end of the night, my feet were really sore but it didn't make the smile on my face go anywhere. This had to have been the best night of my life. I felt like a princess, I was treated like a princess, and I laughed and ate like a king!

*****

When the limousine pulled up to my house, all the lights were on and I caught my mother peering out of the window, trying to camouflage herself in with the curtains. I laughed. Jack and I kissed goodbye in the limo before he walked me to my door.

"Thank you so much for tonight. The entire night was perfect!" I told him. He kissed me briefly on my lips then once on my forehead.

"You deserve to be happy," he said. I gave him a quick kiss on the cheek and waved to the limo, maybe Emily had seen me.

I opened my front door. My mother was right there to greet me with a huge smile on her face.

"And? How was it?" she asked. It looked as though she was holding her breath. I smiled at her and took her hand.

"It was amazing!" I said.

I went to the couch with her and we sat

down. I gave her a full play by play of my entire evening.

Chapter 8

"So?" Emily said out of the blue. "Anything new at home?" she asked. I looked at her with my eyebrows creased in confusion. "Well, you haven't been telling me about your dreams anymore and if you've seen "you know who."" she said as she lowered her voice. I laughed.

"Maybe that's because nothing's been happening! Since prom, Arnold has been staying away, or at least he's being quiet," I said as to not jinx myself.

"Oh," Emily replied. "That's good." She sounded disappointed.

"Were you hoping for a different answer? I'm confused," I said with a giggle.

"Oh no! I'm happy he's leaving you alone, I was just wondering," she said.

We were sitting outside on her front porch reading every book that we have opened throughout the school year. Finals were coming up in one week and we wanted to be sure that we were graduating.

"Do you want to switch?" I asked Emily as I shoved a pile of about seven books towards her while I eyed her pile.

"Yep," she replied and she pushed her pile over to me using two hands. We both laughed.

We've been going to school together since kindergarten, so we've studied together for everything we've ever had to study for. We had a good rhythm; she reads her stuff, I read my own and then we discuss it. It's always worked for us.

"Let's go out tonight!" Emily said. She slammed her book closed. "We've been studying for hours and hours for days! We need a break!" she announced. I laughed at her spontaneous decision.

"Okay! I'm in!" I replied.

"Good," she said as she picked up her phone and dialed out.

"Jack? Hi, it's Emily," she started. My mouth dropped. *I could've called him*, I thought.

"You, me and Tina are going out tonight, okay? Wanna go to Jupiter's?" she asked then waited a second for his reply.

"Okay, you call Joel and we will meet you there at eight," she said then hung up. I started laughing at her again.

"You're acting crazy!" I told her.

"I need a break!" she repeated then reopened her book. I shook my head and continued studying the book that I was reading.

*****

"Hey guys!" Emily shouted over the music when Jack and Joel showed up. Jack came around to my side and put his arm around me then planted a kiss on my cheek. It was a loud kiss. I looked up at him confused.

"What? I missed you," he said then he gave me a real kiss. I welcomed it and wrapped my arms around his neck.

"Get a room!" Emily shouted. I pulled away and looked down embarrassed. Emily laughed and walked by us grabbing my arm in the process.

"Let's find a table," she said. We found one right near the dance floor. We all sat down.
"First things first," Emily said. "There are a few rules for tonight," she announced. "The first rule is: no kissing!" she said as she eyed Jack and myself. Again, my eyes went down in embarrassment. Jack smiled and shook his head.

"Second," she continued, "there will be no mention of finals! And third: we all have to have a lot of fun tonight!" she finished and held her glass of soda up high so we could all make a toast. We all cheered and tapped each other's glass with our own.

Emily and I got up to dance for a while. They were playing great songs. Every time we started to walk back to our table, the DJ played another good song so we continued to dance. We kept meeting up with friends from school so our dancing circle continued to grow. Eventually, Jack and Joel joined us on the dance floor.

Jack spoke directly into my ear to tell me that he was going to get another soda and had to repeat it twice before I understood. He started to push his way through the crowd, when he was suddenly thrown back into our dancing circle of friends. He stood up, swore and charged into another boy sending that boy flying onto the dance floor with Jack on top of him. Jack punched him three times in the face but the other boy managed to push him off and jump on top of Jack. I was yelling for them to stop. I ran around to the other side of them and saw the boy's face. Under the blood and swelling eye was the boy from the school dance the night he and Jack fought. The crowd pulled him off of Jack and Jack stood up.

"What the hell dude?" Jack yelled.

"You cost me a lot of money that night!" he yelled as he tried to charge towards Jack again but the crowd held him back.

"Let it go dude, it's over," Jack said and he took my hand and we walked away. I grabbed Emily's hand as we left and Joel followed.

"Sorry to have ruined your night Emily," Jack said sarcastically when we got outside.

"Hey, no problem! I'm pumped now! Let's go crash a karate class!" she replied with her fists up. Jack couldn't help but laugh; we all did. We decided to call it a night and walk home together.

*****

I couldn't sleep when I got home. I tried for a couple of hours and I tossed and turned. I decided that I would take a shower; maybe the hot water would tucker me out.

After my shower, I still couldn't sleep. I thought of Jack being thrown around by that boy and I thought of finals and graduation. My mind wouldn't let me rest. I got out of bed and I went to my mother and father's room. I quietly woke up my mother.

"Mom," I whispered and gave her a little nudge. She sat up fast.

"What's wrong?" she said loudly.

"Shhhhhh," I told her. "I can't sleep. I was wondering if maybe you'd let me have one of your sleeping pills, just for tonight?" I asked. She thought about it for a second and decided to give me one. She reached into her night stand drawer and shook one pill out of the bottle and handed it to me.

"Make sure you go straight to bed when you take this," she warned.

"I will, Mom; thank you," I said and I gave her a kiss on the cheek before walking out of her room.

I woke up in a cold sweat just as Holly pulled on my arm in my nightmare. *Thanks for the jinx Emily*, I thought with a smirk. I was surprised to see that it was morning. I haven't slept a full night in a long time. I looked down as I reached for my top sheet to wipe the sweat off of my face, when I noticed that there was hair everywhere. It was the colour of my hair. My eyes moved frantically over all of the hair on my bed. My eyes rested on a metal object right beside me. I lifted it; it was an electric shaver still plugged into the wall.

"No, no, no, no, no!" I repeated louder and louder. I was frozen in place; my arms wouldn't move to let my hand feel my head. I looked at all of the hair again and reached down to grab some. I held it in my hands for a second while tears started flowing from my eyes. I reached up and felt my head; some parts were soft like when Jack first gets a haircut and some parts, like around my ears and the back of my head, were still long. I let out a gut wrenching scream that wouldn't stop. The more I touched my head and saw the hair on my bed and in my hands, the louder and longer my screams were.

I was sobbing by the time my parents reached my bedroom door. My father ran to me, took the razor out of my hand, threw it to the floor and took me into his arms to hug me. My mother stopped at my bedroom doorway, her eyes were wide with terror. When our eyes met, she cried with me. My father let go of me to give my mother some room on my bed to hug me too. Together, the three of us hugged until my sobs subsided.

"Tina, honey, why did you do this?" my father asked. I looked up at him and started to cry again. He hugged me.

"Tina, I don't understand," my mother questioned.

"Neither do I," I said in between sobs.

171

"Why would he do this to me?" I asked.

"Who?" my father asked and stood up with his fists at his waist.

"Arnold," I replied. My mother let go of my hand and stood up. My father looked at her with his eyes full of questions.

"Who's Arnold?" he asked.

"Dad! He's the spirit who's been haunting me! He threw me out of my window!" I shouted. He smirked.

"You believe this?" he said when he saw that I wasn't laughing.

"Yes! Why are you looking at me like that?" I asked my father when the smirk left his face and was replaced with a blank stare.

"Mom?" I asked still looking at my father.

"I'm sorry, Tina," she said. "This has gone completely out of hand," she said and walked out of my room; my father followed.

I jumped out of my bed and gathered up all of my hair and threw it into my garbage can. I walked over to the mirror. My image made me cry all over again. It looked so much worse than it felt. There were patches everywhere. I bent down and picked up the shaver. The only thing left to do would be even it out. I lifted it and shaved off the remaining long strands. When I was finished, I pulled the shaver's plug out of the wall and placed it back on the floor. I went to my closet and pulled out a hat; it was pink in colour with a ribbon on the front. I had bought it last October for Breast

Cancer Awareness.

I went to my dresser and pulled out the most feminine coloured clothes that I could find. I didn't have many. I decided on a black pair of leggings with a pink t-shirt. I pulled out a black cardigan sweater from my closet but left the sweater open to show off the pink underneath. As I stood staring at the reflection in my mirror, my bedroom door was thrown open. Standing in my bedroom doorway with her arms crossed was my mother along with two paramedics.

"This is my daughter; please do what you have to do," was all she said. She said it in a stern voice but I saw the pain in her eyes when she said it and also when she walked away.

The two men came into my room and came straight for me, each taking me by an arm.

"Stop! What are you doing? Where are you taking me?" I demanded.

"Your Mom thinks that you might be a little sick, that's all. We are just taking you to get checked," one of the men said. He had a beautiful smile.

"I'm not sick!" I reassured him.

"We just need you to get checked. When they see that you are fine, you can come straight back home," he promised.

"No!" I told them while I tried to pull away.

They were much stronger than I was but I wasn't going to let them take me. I let my legs drop and my bottom hit the floor. With my heel, I kicked the man to my left in the shin three times before he let my arm go. Then, I turned to the other man and tried to do the same but he knew it was coming so he blocked my kicks. I tried throwing myself to the floor, like my younger siblings did when they didn't get their way, but the one paramedic on my right took me by both my arms and stood me up with my back pressed against his front. When he had me pinned against him, he twisted my arm so my wrist faced upwards. The other paramedic came around, put a needle in my vein and pressed the serum into it. It didn't take long before I was seeing double and I couldn't use my legs.

I was dragged out of my room, lifted down the stairs and out of the front door. They placed me on a stretcher and strapped me in. I closed my eyes. I didn't want to see who was watching; I didn't want to see if my sister was around and I never wanted to see my mother again. I kept my eyes closed until we reached the hospital and they wheeled me into the psychiatric ward. When they unstrapped me and placed me onto a hospital bed in what would be my room, I opened my eyes for the first time. The two paramedics had already left and a nurse stood above me.

"I hear you gave the two hottest paramedics in Cornwall a hard time?" she asked. I rolled my eyes. "Okay," she said with a smile. "We won't talk boys."

I turned my head to look out of the

174

window. We were on the third floor so I didn't see cars or people, but I did see the tops of a couple of other buildings. I turned all of my focus on how many buildings I could see.

"You don't have to lie down if you don't want to. You can sit up if you'd like," the nurse offered. "My name is Nurse Jesse," she said. Jesse looked like she may have been in her early thirties. She was cute, not pretty but there was something about her that drew you to her. She had medium length light brown hair; it ended just above her shoulders. Her eyes were blue; you didn't have to stare at her to see how beautiful her eyes were. And she looked to be on the short side.

I didn't reply. I just lied there, staring at the tops of the buildings.

"Okay, but if you feel that you want to sit up or walk down the hallway, you are more than welcome to," she said. She walked away from me and I followed her with just my eyes. She went to the far end of my room, which wasn't that far but it was the furthest from me, and she sat at a desk that faced me.

"Ugh, you're not leaving?" I asked in the rudest tone that I have ever used.

"Oh no, honey, I'm your nurse. I will be with you during my shifts for your entire stay here," she said with a smile.

"For my entire stay here? You say it like I'm on vacation!" I shouted to her. "I just want to go home!"

"It's not so bad here, sweetheart, I promise. We have a TV room and a game room. There is a young lady just next door who is about your age. We know that you don't want to be here, I mean, who does? Everyone would rather be at home but if you have no choice, I say make the best of it!" she said in an upbeat tone.

"No, I'm sorry, I have finals coming up and I need to study. There is so much that I need to do before graduation and I can't do any of it in here!" I shouted again. I sat up, hopped out of the bed and went to the door. Jesse met me at the door before I got to it.

"We can go for a walk down the hall, Tina, but that's as far as we go," she said, her eyes grew stern as she glared at me.

"I'm going home!" I said and shoved her out of my way. She lost her balance which made it easy for me to open the door and run.

I ran down the hall. I looked back once to see Jesse emerge from the room when "bam" I ran right into two male nurses. I bounced back and fell onto my bottom. They came one on either side of me and picked me up by my arms to bring me back to my room. I kicked and screamed all of the way there. They were too strong for me to get away from. They pulled me up onto the bed and laid me down. Still using force to hold me down on the bed as I kicked and screamed, they inserted another needle into my arm. Once again, it didn't take long before I was seeing double. I let the serum take over and fell asleep.

*****

I slept for a long time. It was morning when I woke up. Nurse Jesse was there again. Apparently, I slept through an entire shift change. I sat up and rubbed my eyes. My stomach was growling loud and it was painful. Jesse must have heard my belly because she stood up immediately when my belly growled and went to the door to grab my tray of breakfast.

"You must be hungry," she said with a smile. "Eat, dear. You'll feel better."

"Thanks," I replied and pulled the little table closer to reach my tray better. The food was still hot and it was all foods that I enjoyed. There was a boiled egg with a slice of bran toast, orange juice and milk, along with a bowl of cereal. I ate everything on my plate. It wasn't delicious like the way my mother would make it but it was good. I pushed the table with the tray on it away and looked up at Jesse; she was staring at me.

"Can I go home today?" I asked.

"I don't think so but you do have an appointment with our psychiatrist in a half an hour. If he feels you are well enough to go home then absolutely," she said, again with that smile. It was like nothing bothered her.

"Can I go to the bathroom?" I asked her.

"Of course you can, dear," she replied and directed me to the left where I had my own private washroom.

*****

"Hello, Tina, my name is Dr. Smythe," the psychiatrist greeted me as soon as I walked into his office.

"Have a seat anywhere you'd like," he told me as he motioned his hand around the room.

I looked around. He had a desk on the far wall with two chairs in front of it. He had a black leather couch, a love seat and a chair in the center of the room, accented with a black coffee table and two end tables. I chose the leather chair; I didn't want him to sit beside me.

Dr. Smythe was in his fifties and had a head of snow white hair. His eyes were a crystal blue and he was wearing an expensive suit and really shiny shoes.

"What brings you to my office, my dear? Is there anything that you'd like to talk about today?" he asked. What brings me to his office? Really?

"Two really strong paramedics brought me to your office, sir," I replied. I have never been so rude to anyone in my life nor have I been so upset.

"Why do you think they brought you here?" he asked, ignoring my sarcasm. I looked down. I didn't deserve this; I didn't deserve to be here.

"Do you want to talk about something different? I'm here for you to talk to, so we can talk about anything you'd like," he told me.

"Fine, my Mom called and had me brought here," I spat.

"And why do you think she did that?" he asked.

"Because she thinks that I shaved my head," I explained.

"Did you?" he asked. He never looked at me when he asked a question.

"No!" I shouted. "Why on earth would I shave my head?" I asked.

"Who do you think shaved your head?" he asked ignoring my question. I opened my mouth to answer then stopped myself.

"I don't know but it wasn't me," I told him.

"I don't want you to tell me anything that you don't want to tell me, but if you tell me the truth, it could mean that you go home faster," he said or more like blackmailed.

"I don't know what you want me to say. I woke up and my hair was gone," I replied.

He nodded and waited to see if there was anything else that I wanted to say.

"Okay, same time tomorrow. Have a good day, Tina." He dismissed me with a smile.

I parted my lips to ask him why we were done, but quickly decided against it and got up and left the room. I went back to what they called my room and climbed into the bed and under the covers. I curled up into the fetal position and tried really hard to fall asleep. Jesse sat there but she didn't say anything to me. There was a knock on the door and Jesse went to it. She thanked whoever was on the other side and closed the door. She came over to my bed and handed me a little cup of pills and a glass of water.

"What is this?" I asked holding the cup out in disgust.

"They are your pills, honey," she answered with a short giggle.

"I don't want pills," I replied, still holding them out to her.

"You need to take them. Dr. Smythe's orders," she said.

I looked into the little cup at three small green pills.

"Are they all the same pill?" I asked.

"Yes, it's the recommended dose for you, sweetheart," she said again with a smile. I closed my eyes and poured the cup into my mouth and washed them down with the glass of water.

Nurse Jesse took the glass and small cup from me and brought them to the door where she set them on a small table. She put on a glove. With her gloved hand, she walked over to me and asked me to open my mouth. I looked at her questioningly but did as I was told. She gently put her index finger in my mouth and slid it all around; under my tongue, around my teeth and at the roof of my mouth. When she didn't find anything, she smiled at me and told me that I had done a good job and went over to the garbage to remove her glove. I sat there with my mouth still open in disbelief that she had just done that to me. She saw my expression.

"It's mandatory, dear. A lot of patients pretend to take the pills but spit them out later," she explained. I nodded my head and looked away. She handed me some clothes.

"Here you go. Just put these on and I will take the clothes that you have on and put them in a bag for your discharge date," she told me. I didn't move nor did I take her clothes. "It's the rules for this floor, sweetheart. I promise to keep your clothes safe," she said with a smile.

I took the clothes and went to my washroom and changed. They kind of looked like light green scrubs but made with a cheaper material. I was also given a pair of panties and a pair of socks with slippers. The slippers had a rubber sole.

"Can I leave my bra on?" I called from the washroom.

"Yes, you may," she replied. I came out of the washroom and handed her my clothes. "Your hat too," she said pointing to my head. I reluctantly removed my hat and handed it to her.

My hands instinctively went to my head. I rubbed the soft stubble that was left of my hair and a few tears escaped my eyes. I turned and went to the bed and climbed under the covers. I spend the rest of the day under them.

Chapter 9

My father visited me at the hospital on the third day that I had been admitted. My mother tried to come in with him, but I didn't let her.

"Don't let her in Nurse Jesse. I don't want to see her!" I shouted as I stared at my mother.

"Don't be mean, honey. She misses you," my father told me. His eyes kept moving from me to my mother; he looked like he felt that he was put in the middle of an argument.

"Don't be mean? Really, Dad? What she did was mean!" I replied. I turned my back to my mother. He let it go. He gave Jesse a nod and Jesse asked my mother to wait in the lobby. My mother went to the lobby without a fight.

"So, have you spoken with Emily and Jack? Do they know that I am in here?" I asked my father to break the silence.

"I don't know, honey. Your mother deals with that stuff," he replied.

"Well, did they call?" I pushed.

"I haven't spoken with them," he said.

"So you don't know if they know anything?" I asked again.

"No, honey, I don't know," he said with a hint of annoyance in his words.

"Fine," I said and I changed the subject. I

asked how my sister and her puppy were doing and how my baby brother was. He would be turning one in just a few short weeks.

My father didn't say much; he mostly just answered any questions that I had asked. When I ran out of questions, and I had a lot of them, he stood up to leave. He gave me a gigantic hug and told me he'd be back soon to visit again. He didn't say anything but I knew that he was disappointed that I didn't want to see my mother.

*****

Two weeks had past and I was still in the hospital. My father came back to visit me a handful of times; he was told by Nurse Jesse not to come too often as it may interfere with my healing process. My mother tried to visit twice but I asked Jesse not to let her into my room. I was taking my medication daily and I have not had one dream of Arnold since I was admitted into this ward. I welcomed sleep. In the last few months, sleep had become my enemy so this was a blessing in disguise. I felt better; I had an abundance of energy and my hair was starting to grow back. It was maybe an inch longer since it was shaved. I missed Emily and Jack so much. I haven't spoken with them and I still had no idea if they knew where I was. I missed finals but Nurse Jesse reassured me that the school would let me do them later considering my circumstances.

I did meet the girl who was next door to

183

me; she was released the week before but I was able to talk to her for a day. She was really nice; her name was Angela. She was tall with straight brown hair that went to the middle of her back and she had brown eyes. We spent her last day here playing different board games and we watched three movies. Although I hardly knew her and was happy that she got to go home, I selfishly wished she was still in the hospital with me.

I had grown to accept my appointments with Dr. Smythe, but I still refused to tell him anything about the Trepherd family. I wanted to go home and I knew my story made me sound like I was crazy. Instead, I would make up lies and tell him that it was friends messing with me or maybe it was the neighbors but, since my stories never made sense, I was stuck here until they did. I had to admit that I loved the sleep and the company wasn't so bad. I didn't make any friends but I did have acquaintances. I would see the same people every day in the game room or the TV room and I'd nod my head at them or give them a quick "hello" when I'd see them.

When Jesse's shift was over, I had a different nurse but always the same two: Nurse Jesse and Nurse Susie. Nurse Susie was nice but I preferred Jesse. Susie was in her forties, she was short and plump; she had short curly hair that was reddish in colour and she was sweet. She always had a smile on her face and she was always nice to me. Nurse Jesse and I became friends. I knew our friendship would end when I was discharged but until then I loved telling her all about my life with Jack and how crazy Emily was. Jesse always listened to me and smiled and sometimes she even gave me some advice.

*****

"What shall we talk about today?" Dr. Smythe asked me.

"I guess we could talk about the ghosts that I thought were haunting me," I said. *Here goes nothing,* I thought to myself. Dr. Smythe looked up with interest. I continued.

"I understand now after being here for two weeks that it was all my imagination. I was extremely stressed over finals and my prom and of course graduating from high school that I wasn't sleeping very well. I've had time to put thought into my stories since I've been here and I realized that all the characters that I perceived to be ghosts were solely the names of my little sister's imaginary friends," I said all at once. Dr. Smythe nodded his head while he looked down at his pad of paper.

"You seem to be sure of that," he replied.

"I am. I haven't had any interactions with any of the ghosts that I thought were messing with me at home. Surely, a hospital door wouldn't stop them from visiting me here," I told him as I tried very hard to make eye contact. He continued to look down at his notepad.

"You honestly believe that you made these characters up in your mind?" he questioned.

"No, I believe that I stole the characters from my little sister who says they are her imaginary friends," I reminded him.

"Who do you believe shaved your hair off?" he asked, still not making eye contact with me.

"I have to assume that it was me. I was really tired, but I couldn't sleep so I asked my Mother for a sleeping pill. She gave me one. I may have sleepwalked over to the washroom and took the shaver out and brought it to my room. It was done extremely poorly; it could have passed for something done in someone's sleep. I was really stressed out with everything that was on my plate," I said. I was pretty much begging him to believe me.

He wrote some notes down and he asked me a few questions about how I was adjusting to my surroundings and what my goals were. I answered those questions as truthfully as I could.

"I'm impressed, Tina. Definite progress was shown today," he said as he looked up at me and smiled.

I couldn't help but feel good about myself even though most of what just came out of my mouth were lies. I smiled back and stood up; I knew our session was over. I took a habit of staring at the clock while I sat in his office so one glance at the clock and I already knew that he would say.

"Same time tomorrow," Dr. Smythe said. I

smiled to myself and left his office.

I walked slowly back to my room. Jesse had decided to trust that I would come straight back to my room after my appointments, so she gave me the privilege of having a two minute walk of alone time for the past two days and it felt wonderful.

I entered my room and Jesse greeted me with a smile.

"Wanna go and watch a movie?" I asked her.

"Sure," she said and stood up, "after you." She gestured her arms to point towards the door.

I walked out of the room with Jesse trailing right behind me. After a thirty second walk, we entered the TV room. It was empty. I smiled; I loved not having to decide with someone else what they felt like watching. I went through the movies and chose a romantic comedy. We sat together and watched the movie from start to finish with no interruptions.

*****

"I'm going to go and see about your pills," Jesse said when we reached my room.

"Okay," I told her as I hopped onto my bed.

Jesse left the room and came back about five minutes later. She was smiling.

"No pills today!" she said happily. "That means that you are on your way to recovery and should be going home soon!" she said as she clapped her hands. I hopped off the bed and hugged Jesse.

"This is great! I'll be able to see Jack and Emily soon! Oh and my sweet little Heidi!" She did a little victory dance with me and then we decided to head over to the game room for the rest of the day.

*****

"Run Holly!" I shouted as I ran through the forest. I looked over and Holly was running with all of her might beside me; her little hand was holding mine so tightly. I reached down as we continued to run and I lifted her into my arms. I held her close to me and ran the fastest that I had even run.

"Is he close?" I yelled into Holly's ear.

"Yes," she yelled back and buried her face into the crook of my neck. Just then, I tripped on a root that was sticking out of the ground. It was so dark that I couldn't see it. I dropped Holly, but I screamed at her to run. She stayed and pulled and tugged on my hand but it was too late. I looked back just as Arnold reached down to grab me.

I woke up screaming. I was drenched in sweat. Nurse Susie ran to my side.

"Are you okay, dear?" she asked with her hands on my shoulders.

"Yes, I just had a bad dream," I said and I jumped off of my bed and started to strip the sheets off of it.

"I'll do that, dear; you go and sit on that chair," she instructed.

I walked to the washroom instead and splashed cold water on to my face. *The pills must have stopped my dreams from happening*, I thought to myself. After a few minutes, Susie was knocking on my door.

"Are you okay? Your bed is freshly made," she said through the crack. I opened the door and walked out. She stopped me and held me by my arms. "Are you okay?" she repeated.

"Yes, I'm fine. I actually don't even remember my dream," I lied. I crawled back into bed and pretended to fall back to sleep. I laid there awake with my eyes closed and waited for the nurse's shift change.

When Jesse came in, I pretended that I was just waking up. She greeted me with a smile.

"Did you sleep well?" she asked. I saw Nurse Susie from the corner of my eye shake her head "no." I sighed heavily.

"I had a bad dream but I don't even remember it," I said. She nodded her head. Suzie gave Jesse her notes from her shift and they chatted quietly for a few minutes at their desk. When they were finished, Nurse Suzie gathered her things and prepared to leave. We both said "goodbye" as she left.

*****

"I'm reading here that you didn't sleep well last night," Dr. Smythe observed. I rolled my eyes but he didn't see me.

"I slept fine. I had a nightmare but I can't even remember it," I told him.

"Okay. Is there anything that you want to talk about today?" he asked me.

"Not really. I guess I told you everything yesterday," I said.

He went over his usually daily routine with me. He talked about different exercises I could do to test my brain. Brain teasers mostly. I liked those so I listened attentively.

"You did really well yesterday. So well, that you will be discharged in two days. Friday will be your last day and Saturday morning your father will be here to pick you up. He's already been notified. We will still have two more meetings together, but all in all I think that your stay here did you some good," he announced in his formal tone. I couldn't wipe the smile from my face. I wished that I had told him all of this during my first week here.

I returned to my room with a huge smile and gave Nurse Jesse my news. She couldn't be happier for me.

*****

Home. Was it home? Would I ever feel at home again in that house? My mother betrayed me and I knew Arnold was waiting for me. But I still smiled when my father arrived to pick me up.

"Hi Dad!" I said and I gave him a big kiss on his cheek. "Nice to see you!" I told him.

"It's nice to see you too!" he replied. "Your Mom can't wait to see you either," he told me.

"Oh, why?" I asked. My mother wanted me out of the house so badly that she had me removed from it. *Why would she be happy to see me?* I thought to myself.

"Your Mom did what she thought was best, honey. She felt horrible and still does but she has all these plans for you and her to do together to help make it up to you," he explained.

"I'm not interested, Dad. I didn't even get a warning or anything. Instead, I had my door swung open by two huge paramedics who dragged me somewhere that I didn't want go," I said stubbornly.

"Would you have stayed if your Mom had warned you? Or would you have run away to hide from them?" he asked.

"I guess we will never know since I wasn't trusted with that decision," I replied.

Jesse was there to see me go. She gave me a really big hug and wished me luck in my future. I thanked her for being there for me.

My father and I made our way to the car. I had no luggage. I wore the clothes that I had given them during my first night there. That was all I had. We both got into the car and drove home, which was only about five minutes away.

My mother was standing outside waiting for me when we pulled into the driveway. I sighed and my father looked over at me. He seemed incredibly uncomfortable with my annoyance towards my mother.

"Hi, honey!" my mother said as she greeted me.

"Hey," was my reply. I walked passed her open arms and went into the house. There she was!

"Heidi! I missed you so much!" I called to her as soon as I laid eyes on her.

"Tina!" she yelled my name perfectly and ran over to me for the biggest hug of her life.

After I showered Heidi with kisses and hugs, I made my way up the stairs to my room. When I reached the top and looked into my room, I wanted to scream. My door had been removed! I took a few breaths, walked through my doorway and sat on my bed. I looked around; everything else seemed to be the same way that I had left it. I laid my head back on to my pillow and I stared at my ceiling. A few minutes later, my parents were at my doorway; they didn't say anything.

"Where's my door and why did you remove it?" I asked directing the question towards my mother. I sat up and glared at her with so much hate burning through my eyes that she took a step back. She looked up at my father, but there wasn't any hate in my heart. I still loved my mother very much; I could never hate my mother. I just really didn't understand her.

"We were told that it would be best," she stammered.

"And when were you told that it could be put back on?" I questioned without batting an eye.

"I'll find out," was all she said and she walked away from my room. My father shook his head and walked out of my room too.

I didn't like treating my mother this way but I have never lied to her... Ever! She had no reason not to believe me and, instead of trying to figure things out, she had me committed. It will take a while before I could talk to her again. I decided to close my eyes and take a nap. I never minded having my door opened at night but during the day was extremely uncomfortable. It took a while but, after what seemed like an eternity, I managed to fall asleep for a bit.

*****

When I woke up, I noticed that there were some papers at the end of my bed. I sat up and grabbed them. They were my make-up dates for my finals! I was taking them the following week starting on Monday.

I threw the covers off of me and jumped out of bed. I gathered all of my books from school and started reading and studying them.

I read and made all sorts of notes for hours before I decided to take a break. I went downstairs and out the front door and I sat on my front steps. I could smell supper; my mother was making tacos. That was a sure sign that she felt bad for what she had done. I lost two weeks of my life and I didn't get to graduate with my class. Now, I had to cram two exams in only one day and a half. *She should feel bad*, I thought. I sat on the steps for a while. I watched as the cars drove by and I looked down at the ground every time a neighbor would walk by. I knew that the only reason they were walking by was to get a glimpse at my new hair. I got fed up and went back into the house. My mother called my name just as I started up the stairs.

"Yeah?" I called back.

"Supper is ready. Do you want to come and eat?" she asked. I couldn't see her; she was still in the kitchen preparing supper. My belly was growling but my pride took over.

"No thanks," I said and I went back up to my room and I opened another book.

A little while later, my mother came to my door with a plate of tacos. *Thank goodness!* I thought to myself. I didn't make eye contact with her and she didn't push for attention. She placed the plate at the foot my bed and left my room. I was sitting on my bed with my back against the wall and my knees were up so my legs could hold up the book that I was reading. I quickly put the book down and took the plate. I scarfed down my food with only a few breaths in between. I didn't realize how hungry I was and it was so much better than hospital food.

*****

My teachers were very happy to see me. They seemed to know where I was but they didn't make me feel uncomfortable. My first exam was math. I wasn't nervous about this exam because math was one of my favourite classes. I followed my math teacher, Mr. Walsh, to his classroom. He smiled as he handed me my exam. I gave him a small smile and took a seat. I looked through my exam at all the questions before I started answering them. Once I read through the entire test, I flipped back and started to answer them in order. I looked up a couple of times and Mr. Walsh was staring at me but he must have been in a daze because he didn't notice that we had made eye contact a few times. When I was finished, I stood up and that made Mr. Walsh jump, I held back a giggle but he noticed and smiled.

"I didn't get much sleep last night," he confessed.

"Me neither," I said with a smile. He nodded.

"Well thank you for letting me do the exam," I said and I left his office.

My next exam wasn't scheduled for another two hours so I decided to go home. I thought about calling Emily or Jack but I wasn't ready to talk to them yet. I walked home with my earphones in my ears listening to whatever station I was able to pick up. I wasn't in the mood to go through my playlist.

When I arrived on my street, I could smell something burning but I didn't see any smoke. I walked a little quicker to my house and the smell was getting stronger. I walked around to the back and that's when I saw the smoke. It was coming from my backyard. I put my school bag down and opened the gate. When I went through the gate door, I stopped in my tracks. My mother had made a fire pit in the backyard and was burning all of my clothes. One by one, she was throwing all the pieces of my wardrobe into her fire pit. I ran to her and pulled my sweater out of her hands.

"What are you doing?" I screamed at her.

"Don't yell! Your brother and sister are sleeping," she told me in a calm voice.

"Mom!" I yelled. "Why are you burning my clothes?"

She seemed to have snapped out of a daze.

"You're supposed to still be at school! Why are you home?" she shouted.

"What?" I asked her.

"What am I going to do?" she asked herself and started to cry but she continued to throw my clothes into the fire.

"Stop!" I screamed and I took my clothes that were in her hands away from her. "You can't burn my clothes!" I looked down at what little clothes I had left. "Why are you doing this?" I screamed at her with tears streaming down my face.

"I have to," she said and she fell to her knees and sobbed.

I gathered my small amount of clothes and brought them up to my room. I felt that I needed to check on my siblings while I was upstairs, so I did. They were both fast asleep in their beds. I went back to my room and started folding my clothes and putting them back into my drawers. Just then, my mother came into my room.

"I need those clothes back," she said calmly and went to take them out of my drawer.

"No! Get out of my room!" I yelled. "What's wrong with you?"

"Arnold will be so mad!" she cried and fell to the floor in a fit of hysterics. I froze in place. Arnold will be mad? What? I gave in; I couldn't bear to see her like this.

"Mom, take the clothes," I told her. I helped her take them out of my drawer. She didn't say anything; she just turned around and left my room with a stack of the only clothes that I had left.

I waited for her to finish. When she came back into the house, I went downstairs. She was washing her hands and she was preparing to do the dishes. She was humming a little tune to herself.

"Mom?" I asked as I slowly approached her. She spun around and wore a beautiful smile.

"What are you doing home, dear? I thought you had two finals to do today?" she asked.

"Mom? What were you just doing?" I asked

her. She looked at me confused.

"I was washing my hands and now I'm going to wash the lunch dishes. Why?" she replied.

"No, what were you doing outside?" I asked her. I was talking very slowly and very calmly, which made her look at me like I was crazy.

"I wasn't outside," she said. She turned around to stop the water that was filling the sink for her dishes.

"Yes, you were Mom!" I shouted. She turned to face me.

"I was not! I put Heidi and Tommy down for their naps and then I came downstairs to clean up," she said.

"And what time was that at?" I asked her.

"A few minutes ago; it was at 12:30," she replied.

"Look at the time, Mom." I pointed at the clock that read 1:45 pm. She stared at it and was speechless.

"Mom, you were just outside burning all of my clothes," I told her. She looked at me with a note of recognition.

"I burned all of your clothes? I dreamt that I did that. I didn't actually do it, Tina! It was a dream!" she panicked. I led her to the backyard where the fire was out but the remains were all still out there.

"Did you dream about shaving my head too, Mom? Or how about taking Heidi's puppy and hiding her for two weeks?" I shouted at her. All of my anger and all of my frustrations were coming out all at once.

"I did," she whispered. "I didn't know it was really me when it actually happened. I didn't remember doing it!" she cried.

"You had dreams of doing all of these things and then when they actually happened you didn't stop and think that maybe it was you? Instead, you conveniently passed the blame on to me?" I screamed.

"I'm sorry!" she yelled. "I'm sorry, I didn't know! You kept on with your story of the ghosts in this house so it just made sense to me that you were at fault!" she sobbed. I turned and went back up to my room, leaving my mother sobbing on the charred grass outside.

"Arnold!" I shouted. "Leave my Mom alone!" I looked around frantically as I yelled. "Leave her alone! Do you hear me?" I begged. He didn't appear. "How do I right the wrong for you to leave us alone?" I screamed. I heard my sister stir but she didn't come out of her room. I really wish my door was still intact. I looked around again but there was no sign of him. Then, it hit me. I dropped down to my knees and looked up.

"I forgive you, Arnold! I forgive you for killing me and Holly when I was your wife!" I yelled. "I forgive you, now please go!" I screamed. Tears were streaming down my face. I sat down on the floor and buried my face into my hands and then I heard him. He laughed. I looked up but I didn't see him right away. I hurriedly climbed onto my bed and waited for him.

"Please!" I begged. "Please leave us alone. I forgive you," I whispered. He appeared; he was sitting at the end my bed. He was laughing and shaking his head at me very slowly.

"You don't accept my forgiveness? Well, how do I right the wrong?" I shouted. He shook his head at me again and laughed and that's how he left me. "What am I supposed to do?" I cried. "I can't fix this!"

But all I received in return was his silence.

Chapter 10

"Hey!" Jack said on the other end of the receiver. "I miss you." My heart melted.

"Hi Jack," I replied shyly.

"Where have you been? Your Mom said something about you being out of town with family. What family and why?" he asked. Wow, my mother has a creative mind.

"Jack, I wasn't out of town. There is so much going on right now. Too much to talk about over the phone," I told him.

"Well, let's meet! I can't wait to see you, I miss you so much," he said. I closed my eyes. The last think I wanted him to see was me, with three inches of hair on my head.

"Maybe tomorrow? I'm really busy today," I lied.

"Seriously? I haven't seen you in almost four weeks and you still want to postpone seeing me? I just now hear your voice for the first time and I find out that you were in town this entire time!" He was shouting. I couldn't expect him not to get upset.

"Okay! Okay!" I said. "I was in town but I wasn't home. My Mom had me admitted into the psychiatric ward in the hospital," I admitted.

"What? Holy crap! Why did she do that?

Why didn't she tell me?" he asked quickly.

"She was probably embarrassed about what she had done. I'm more embarrassed for the reason she did it," I said in almost a whisper.

"Why did she do it?" he asked quietly.

"I woke up with my hair shaved off," I said as I started to cry. "It's growing back but not very fast," I told him.

"Who did it?" he asked.

"That's the kicker. The shaver was placed in my hand while I was sleeping so it looked like I had done it. When my parents asked why I did it, I blamed it on Arnold, right? I mean why wouldn't I?" I waited for his agreement.

"I would have thought the same," he said.

"Good! Now, are you ready for the kicker?" I asked.

"Yeah, who did it?" He was getting antsy.

"My Mom," I said point blank.

"What the hell?" He pretty much yelled in my ear.

"Everything's being twisted around over here. I hate it. I hate being here. My Mom is so confused, she's been doing all these things but she doesn't remember doing them." I was pouring everything out into the receiver when all I really wanted was for Jack to hold me in his arms.

"Maybe you should have her admitted!" he said sarcastically. I smirked.

"I thought about it. But I know that it's Arnold who's making her do everything," I told him. "I'd love to see you, Jack. Maybe we can get together but I'm really shy about my new hair doo," I joked, sort of.

"I love you. With or without hair. I'm coming over," he said then hung up before I could say anything else.

I hurriedly got dressed. I put a little more makeup on than usual to intensify my femininity. But I still wore a ball cap. I went downstairs to wait for him. Skittles was at my feet.

"Good morning, Skittles," I said and patted her on the head. Sure enough, when I looked up, Heidi was right there beside her puppy.

"Hey sweet girl!" I told her and I picked her up and swung her around as I gave her a hug. Skittles barked and jumped up at me, scratching at my legs to let Heidi go. I put her down.

"I didn't hurt her, silly you!" I pet her again. Heidi laughed and ran away. Skittles followed.

My mother refused to make eye contact with me since the discovery of her sabotaging my life. My father took me out the day after she burned all of my clothes for a new wardrobe, but because my parents didn't have a lot of money I had to limit myself to only three shirts, one sweater and two pairs of pants. My dad promised that we would go back out next week after his paycheck and get a couple more things.

I managed to get all of my finals done during that week. I didn't think I was going to be able to, especially the one right after my mother burned my clothes but I sucked it up and went to it. I figured that since they had already postponed them once, I couldn't be greedy and ask for another extension.

My mother was in the kitchen preparing a roast beef in the slow cooker for that night's supper. She didn't turn around when I entered the kitchen.

"Jack is coming to get me Mom; I don't know when I'll be back. We have a lot to catch up on seeing that I was out of town visiting family members," I said sarcastically.

She stopped cutting her carrots, took a breath and then continued cutting.

"That's fine, dear. Enjoy your day," she said without turning around. I walked out. I understood that she thought that she was helping me, but the fact that she refused to tell the truth to people to save herself the embarrassment infuriated me.

I sat on the front porch until I saw Jack in his mother's car come to pick me up. I hopped off the last step to meet him. He jumped out of the car and we met in the driveway. He hugged me so hard my feet were off the ground.

"I missed you so much!" he said and he bent down to kiss me. I kissed him back and wrapped my arms as tightly as I could around him. He stepped back to look at me. "You are beautiful no matter what," he said and he made sure our eyes met. I nodded. I just wanted my hair back.

We walked around to the passenger side of

the car and he opened the door for me. I got in and buckled my seatbelt and waited for him to get in. I looked up at the house and my mother was standing in the window watching us. She didn't seem to notice or care that I could see her.

"Weird," Jack said when he noticed what I was looking at. "What is she doing?" he asked when my mother didn't move or blink for that matter.

"I have no idea. It's the first time she even looks at me since I was discharged," I told him.

He backed out of the driveway. I kept my eyes on my mother. It wasn't until we were out of the driveway that she turned around.

"Where are we going?" I asked. He smiled.

"Well, first things first! We have to go and see Emily," he said. I smiled. I missed her.

"Did you tell her about my hair?" I asked. My hands went to the back of my neck. Jack took my hand from my neck and held it.

"No, but do you think she'll judge you?" he asked me.

"No, but she'll be shocked." I looked down until we arrived at her place.

"Does she know we're coming?" I asked when there was no answer at the door.

"No," he laughed. "I just thought that with you gone, she was bored." I nudged him with my elbow and I giggled. "What?" he laughed while he rubbed his arm. I shook my head at him. I missed that smile.

"Hey!" Emily said as she came around from the back. She heard the knock but didn't know who was knocking.

"Oh hey Jack," she said. And then she looked at me. "Tina?" she asked. "Where have you been? You cut your hair? Take your hat off, let me see!" she said with a smile as she tried to grab my hat. When I backed away, she stopped smiling. "What's wrong? You leave for a month and I can't see your doo?" she kidded.

"Emily, Tina wasn't gone visiting family; she was here at the hospital, in the psychiatric ward," Jack explained.

"What?" Emily asked.

The three of us went to the back yard and sat around on her patio furniture and I explained everything to them. They were both speechless.

"I'm telling you, Arnold has some sort of hold on my Mom," I explained. They agreed with me but had no advice. We sat there in silence for a bit. Every now and then, one of us would ask a question or suggest something.

"And when you forgave him, he just laughed?" Emily asked.

"Yes. So now I have to figure out what the wrong is; what he's done to me as his wife, so I can make it right," I told them. They nodded and we continued to discuss the information that I had.

"I'm getting hungry, wanna go for lunch?" Jack asked. We both said "yes" and spent the rest of the day catching up.

*****

"Okay, Mom," I said when I entered the kitchen. She was preparing a salad for supper. It had been a few weeks since I told Jack and Emily all about my stay at the hospital and my mother doing things that she didn't remember. It was time that we talked about it.

She spun around to look at me with a confused expression.

"Arnold. Does that name mean anything to you?" I asked her.

"No, honey, just what you say about him," she replied.

"You never met him or heard him talk to you?" I pressed.

"No," she said and she turned around to continue cutting the vegetables for the salad.

"Mom, we need to figure this out. You need to work with me because if you don't, and with all the evidence I have of the things you've done, I can have you admitted in the psychiatric ward!" I threatened. She turned around again and looked at me as though she was going to punish me but her face softened.

"Okay, I understand how you feel, but honestly the only connection that I have to what's happened is my dreams. There is no man named Arnold in any of them and quite frankly, I still don't believe that there are ghosts in our house," she told me and she went over to the sink to wash her hands.

"So you still think I'm crazy?" I asked her.

"No, but I don't believe in ghosts. Now that we've figured out that it was me doing all these crazy things, it crosses out the possibility of any supernatural activities that could have been happening. Now that we have answers, I think that you should drop the whole ghost act and move on!" she said sternly and moved on to setting the table.

"Okay," I said and walked away. I still haven't been talking to my mother and I've been avoiding her and she's been doing the same to me. That was our first conversation in months. There was no sense in arguing about it. She was dead set against wanting to believe in ghosts and there was no changing her mind.

*****

It was dark, very dark. I was walking alone in the forest. I looked up at all the beautiful stars that were lighting up the sky when, suddenly, I tripped over something and fell flat on my face. I stood up and brushed myself off. I looked back to see what I had tripped over and it was a tree root. I shook it off and I continued to walk through the dark forest. It was unusually quiet. As I continued to walk and look around at all the trees, I stepped on something soft. I picked my foot up and gave it a shake, and then stepped back to see what I had stepped on. It was a small mound of ground. I studied it for a second; it was about three feet wide and six feet long, and right beside it was another small mound of ground about three feet wide and five feet long. As soon as I realized that they were graves, I woke up screaming and drenched in sweat.

"Are you okay?" My mother came rushing into my room. It was obvious that I had woken her up from her sleep.

"I'm really sorry, Mom. I had a horrible dream and I couldn't control the scream," I told her as I pulled the sheets off of my bed. My mother watched me strip my bed.

"You know? You go through an unnecessary amount of sheets," she said then turned and went back to her room.

When my bed was remade and I settled back in, I went over the dream. *Did I just see where I was buried in my past life?* I asked myself. The thought gave me a chill that made me shudder. *At least I didn't have to relive the final moments of that life again*, I thought, but the thought didn't make the eerie feeling go away.

*****

"Do you want to go for a walk through the forest?" I asked Jack when we met up later that week. "I'm pretty sure that I know where Amelia and Holly were buried years ago. I thought that maybe we could just walk by the spot that I dreamt of?" I looked at him and batted my eyes dramatically. He laughed and put his arm around my shoulder.

"Of course, let's go!" he said.

"Where's the closest forest around here?" I asked. He looked down at me with laughter in his eyes.

"You don't know what forest you are dreaming of?" he asked.

"No," I replied honestly. My hope vanished.

"Let's try the one near my house today. We will walk through a few trails and see if it's the one. If it isn't, we'll check the one close to the highway tomorrow," he suggested.

"Thank you!" I said and hugged him.

When we got to the forest, the trail started right at the edge of the road.

"Shall we?" he asked with his hand reaching out for me to grab it.

"Yes," I smiled and took his hand. "What if we get lost?" I asked, as I looked around.

"We'll stick to the trail and if we start to feel uncomfortable, we'll just follow the same trail back," he said.

"Sounds good," I said and I started walking. He was right beside me the whole way. We both looked around as we walked, almost as though we thought someone was going to jump out at us. We were so tense.

We walked for an hour before one of us spoke. It was me.

"This is pointless, I mean think about it. If you were to kill and bury someone, would you bury them close to your place or would you drag them across town to do it?" I asked. I stopped walking and stood in front of him and waited for his reply.

"I'd do the further one," he answered.

"Really? What if you knew you were going to kill yourself? Would you be afraid to get caught?" I challenged.

"No, I guess I wouldn't. You're probably on to something." He thought for a second before continuing. "If we leave right now, we could go to the forest near your place," he teased.

I automatically started running and laughing, when I saw Jack running behind me. I ran faster and Jack kept up while laughing, as loudly as I was. All of a sudden, I did a face plant into the ground. I looked on the ground behind me and my blood ran cold. Jack caught up to me still laughing until he saw what I was staring at.

"Is that the root that's in your dream?" he asked quietly. He grabbed my hand to help me up. I accepted and pulled myself up to stand.

"Yeah," I replied still staring at the root. I looked up and around the forest. "In my dreams, I must be running this way." I pointed in the direction that we were heading to exit the forest. "We must have been running away from him towards the exit," I stated. My eyes drifted to the left. "And over there," I pointed, "is where the bodies are buried." Jack looked over in the direction that I was pointing to.

"Do you want to check it out?" Jack asked. His voice was trembling. I nodded my head.

We both started walking off the trail and towards the left. This made Jack nervous because he kept looking back. I continued to walk, when suddenly it felt like I couldn't breathe. I stopped and took a couple of deep breaths. Jack stopped and waited for me to continue, but it felt as though the butterflies in my stomach were going to explode out and my entire body was shaking. I've never experienced a panic attack before, but I certainly believed that this was one. Without any warning, I turned and went back towards the direction that we had come from. Jack was at my heels, but he didn't say anything, he just followed. When we reached the trail, I continued to leave the forest in a speed walk. I was grateful that Jack didn't ask any questions. After what felt like hours, we finally reached the road. The second that I emerged from the forest, I took a deep breath. It felt like I was in water and just came up for air. Jack put his hand on my shoulder and asked if I was okay.

"I just want to leave," I said and I hopped into his mother's car. He quickly ran around to the driver's side and drove away from the forest. My breathing became easier and the shaking stopped.

"Jeez, that was crazy," I said to Jack as I

checked my pulse on my neck. "I think I had a panic attack," I told him. He nodded but didn't say anything. We drove home in silence.

*****

"Thank you so much for coming over!" I said to France when I greeted her at the door. I booked an appointment with her earlier that week when I knew my family would be out for the evening. They were over at my Aunt Nora and Uncle Mike's place for a few hours.

"My pleasure, dear," she said with a smile. She was staring at my hair; I couldn't blame her, my hair used to be long and beautiful.

"Do you want your cards read?" she asked. We were standing awkwardly together in the kitchen; neither of us really knowing what to do or where to go.

"No, actually. I was hoping that you'd give me some advice. We've been experiencing some crazy things and I really need your expertise on the situation," I told her. She nodded her head and put her hand out, gesturing for me to find a seat. I chose the living room couch. She followed and sat beside me.

"When you are ready, dear, I'm all ears," she said with yet another beautiful smile.

I explained everything to her: from the small incidents like Heidi's hair, right down to my mother shaving my hair off. She listened to everything I said without any interruptions. When I was finished, she stood up and walked around my living room. She looked at the different pictures on the walls and checked out the different figurines on the shelves.

"The spirit Arnold, as you call him, and his wife, Amelia, are in this room as we speak. Amelia says the Arnold will leave you alone as soon as you right the wrong," she started but I cut her off.

"I tried! I told him that, as his wife, I forgive him for taking our lives and he laughed at me," I said almost in a sulk.

"I'm not sure that that would be the wrong that needs fixing. My dear Tina, he was someone very close to you in your past life. He is incredibly upset that you have moved on and he is still stuck in his world. He is capable of doing mean things. The wrong that he needs fixing is not an apology. He won't let Amelia tell me much more. He is very stubborn, but Amelia believes that you have it in you to figure it out and make it right," she explained. She seemed unsatisfied with our session; she looked as though she felt that Amelia could have given me more information but Arnold wouldn't let her.

After she left, I went up to my room and got ready for bed. It was a little early but I figured I'd lie awake and read for a bit.

I heard my parents come it but I didn't go down to greet them. The children had fallen asleep so my parents had to bring them up to their beds. They said "goodnight" to me in passing. I continued to read my book and, without noticing the time, I heard my parents go to bed. I decided to put the book down and close my eyes. I tossed and turned and couldn't fall asleep. I listened for any noises but everyone was asleep, including the dog. I decided to get out of bed and go downstairs for a glass of water, when something in my parents' room caught my attention. I locked my eyes on the object and slowly walked into their room. It was dark but the object was shining to the glare of the bathroom light. Finally, I made out the figure holding the object. It was my mother and the object was a knife. I put my two hands out in front of me to show my mother that I was unarmed.

"Mom, it's just me, Tina," I said calmly. She smiled.

"Tina." And she lunged for me. I screamed and ran out the door closing it behind me.

"Mom! It's just me! Stop!" I screamed but she started banging on the door trying to get out. I had my back pressed against the door, in hopes that my father would wake up and stop her or that she would snap out of it. She continued to bang and scream for me to let her out when I suddenly felt a stabbing pain in my right shoulder. My mother managed to get the knife through the door and into my shoulder. She pulled the knife back and I heard my skin rip with the force that it took her to draw the knife back. I dropped to the floor and I looked up just as the knife pierced through the door again. This time, she screamed my name and repeatedly hit the door with the knife. I turned myself around and faced the door and, using both my feet, I continued to hold the door closed. I reached around with my left hand and pressed on my throbbing shoulder.   The second my fingers touched the opened wound, a shocking pain shot through my body and it reached right down to my toes. I screamed but held my hand there for a minute hoping that it would ease the pain. It didn't. I could tell that it wasn't deep but it hurt and it bled. My mother was still screaming my name and pounding on the door. Blood dripped down the front of my arm and I couldn't help but cry.

"Okay, Mom! You got me, I'm bleeding. You can stop now!" I shouted. I didn't expect the banging to stop but it did. I waited a bit before letting the door go. Why didn't my family wake up to that? He must have had some crazy hold on my entire family for all I knew. A few minutes went by, so I stepped away from the door and looked in. My mother wasn't by the door, only the knife was. I looked in her bed and there she was, fast asleep. I shook my head in astonishment and went downstairs for some ice and a cloth for my shoulder. My PJ sleeve was covered in blood. I managed to take it off and dab the wound with a wet cloth. It felt like my arm was going to fall off, but the stab was only about an inch wide. I texted Jack to see if he'd be able to take me to the hospital. He replied right away and was at my door in less than thirty minutes.

"What the hell is wrong with your Mom?" he yelled and he helped me into the car.

"I'm fine! I just need a couple of stitches. Arnold is mad at me, I assume for having France over tonight, and this is how he deals with his anger," I defended my mother. I felt the same way he did, but I didn't like others talking bad about her.

We drove to the hospital. The hospital was within walking distance, but it was too late at night to do that and I was feeling tired and weak. Jack insisted on dropping me off at the door while he went to park, but I convinced him that I was okay to walk from the parking lot. We parked the car and walked through the entrance together.

The staff asked me what had happened and I came up with the worst lie I've ever used. I told them that I had tripped in the kitchen and fell on a knife. They all gave me crazy "as if" eyes but continued to work on my shoulder regardless.

Jack drove me home after I was stitched up and bandaged. I thanked him for driving me home and to the hospital and waiting with me. He kissed my forehead. I walked into my house. Nobody noticed that I had left. I went upstairs to my room. I had no problem falling asleep this time, I was exhausted.

Chapter 11

I woke up to the sound of my mother screaming at her bedroom doorway. I practically fell out of my bed. Very sleepily, I walked out of my room. I lifted my arm and realized that the cut was much more painful this morning. My mother looked up at me.

"What happened?" she shouted. She bent down and picked up the knife. There was still blood on it. When she looked on the floor in the hallway in front of her doorway and saw all the blood there, she dropped the knife and screamed again. I smirked at her.

"You stabbed me last night. Right through your bedroom door," I said and walked back into my room. My father came up from behind her and followed me into my room.

"What do you mean she stabbed you?" he asked.

"I mean she put that knife through my skin," I sarcastically replied. He looked at me like I was crazy.

"Hey, Mom!" I shouted. "Did you have a dream that you stabbed me?" I asked her in a mocking tone. I stared at my father and waited for her reply.

"Oh no! I did! I dreamt that I stabbed someone through the door because they wouldn't let me out of my room!" She was sobbing. "What's wrong with me?" she cried.

I looked at my father with a knowing glance and then I shook my head.

"But hey, there's nothing weird going on in this house," I sarcastically replied as I turned to make my bed.

"Where did she stab you, Tina?" my father asked in a quiet defeated voice.

"On my shoulder," I said. "But no worries, Jack took me to the hospital because none of you heard me screaming for help; you didn't even know that I left."

"I can't figure out why I didn't wake up," he said and shook his head. "Did you need any stitches?" he asked.

"Six," I said as I continued to make my bed. I refused to look at him because my tough act would have melted and I really wanted to stay strong.

"I'm so sorry, Tina." he said and then walked out of my room to tend to my mother.

*****

"How's your shoulder?" Jack asked through the receiver.

"It's fine, Jack," I said with a smile. I still had some pain medication left from when I broke my leg, so I took one that morning. "I really have to figure out how to right the wrong, Jack. It is complete nonsense over here and what happens when I go to college? Is he gonna follow me?" I asked.

"I don't know. What do you think it could be?" he asked me.

"I don't know, but I have a feeling it has something to do with where the bodies are buried. I think I have to suck it up and go back to them," I said.

"Okay, and then what?" he asked.

"I don't know," I replied. We spoke for a little while longer. After a while, we hung up and Jack came to pick me up.

*****

"Try this again?" Jack asked with his hand extended waiting for mine as we stood in front of the trail through the forest.

"Nope," I said and took his hand anyways. We walked to the protruding root and stepped off the trail towards the graves. I remembered the tree that the graves were beside and I stopped. I looked down but all I saw was flat ground covered in grass. I looked at Jack; he shrugged his shoulders.

"Now what?" I cried. "I'm here! Do you want me here? What do I do now?" I screamed. I wanted Arnold to appear and tell me how to get rid of him, but he stayed away. Jack wrapped his arms around me as I cried. I cried for a while but it didn't accomplish anything. I stood up straight and wiped my eyes with my sleeve.

"We might as well leave," I told Jack and we both turned and left the forest.

*****

I knocked hard on France's door the following morning. I didn't have an appointment and I knew that I was being extremely rude, but this had to end. France opened her door and actually looked pleased to see me.

"Hello Tina, what can I help you with? It's really nice to see you," she said as she opened the door.

"Sorry to drop in unannounced, but I have some new information!" I told her. She nodded and stepped back for me to enter. She led me to her card reading table and motioned for me to sit down. I did. She sat across from me and I told her about the graves.

"Now, how do I find out what they did to him to make him so angry?" I asked her.

"I can ask them," she offered. I nodded my head and waited. France closed her eyes. I waited and looked around for any signs of Amelia and Holly. After a few minutes of nothing, she opened her eyes and apologized.

"They are not here. I will probably have to go to your home," she suggested.

"Yes, yes, anytime! Can you come now?" I asked her. She looked around then down at her appointment book.

"I can!" She seemed excited. "I don't have any appointments booked until early this afternoon!"

We hopped into her car and we were on our way to my house.

"Do you think he'll let them talk?" I asked France as she drove.

"I hope so, but I have no way of knowing for sure until we get to your place. Where are your parents?" she asked.

"At home, I think," I told her. I felt her eyes on me so I looked over at her. "My Mom is sabotaging my life and she could have killed me the other night! They will cooperate!" I predicted. France laughed.

"Determined, aren't we?" she asked.

"Yes! I need my life back," I told her.

When we arrived to my place, both my parents' cars were there.

"Here we go," I said as I opened the car door. France did the same and we went to the front door.

"You might want to wait outside for just a second," I told her and I opened the door slightly and slipped through.

My parents were both in the living room watching television. My father looked up when he saw me.

"Where did you go?" he asked. He looked confused; I don't think he knew that I was even gone.

"I have a medium here. She's going to try to talk to the spirits in this house. Will you cooperate?" I asked.

"She's here right now?" he asked getting up and out of his chair.

"Yes. Mom could have killed me the other night. We either find out if she's being possessed or I have her committed. It's that simple!" I threatened. My father looked at my mother who simply nodded her head.

"Okay, you could leave or you could stay, whatever, but let her do her thing," I said and I turned to open the door to let France in.

"These are my parents: Ron and Janet. Mom and Dad, this is France," I introduced. They shook hands.

"Should we stay or leave?" my father asked her.

"Whatever you'd like," she replied.

"Okay, well we have some shopping that needs to get done," he said and he picked up Heidi, leaving my mother to pick up Tommy. They left within seconds.

I followed France into the kitchen where she sat down and waited for me to do the same. She closed her eyes and waited. I kept my eyes opened and looked around, hoping for some sort of sign.

"Amelia, I can hear you," she said. She was squinting as though she was having a hard time hearing her. "I can't understand," she said shaking her head a little. "Arnold won't let her speak," France explained.

"Holly, is that you?" France continued to try to understand. "It sounds like there is a struggle," she said to me. "Maybe you can say something?" she offered.

"Amelia! If you need me to help right the wrong, please talk louder. Arnold! Let Amelia speak! I know no other way!" I shouted. France put her hand on mine and nodded to me.

"Amelia, I'm listening," she said and listened. I waited patiently for any information. "Tina, they did nothing wrong to Arnold. Arnold abused them for years; leaving them locked up in this house. One day after work, Arnold came home and Amelia had had enough and she called the police. Before the police came, Arnold put them in his car and drove them to the forest. The forest that you've been to," she explained. "He killed them both and buried them. When he arrived home, he'd hoped that they would believe that they ran off, but the police didn't. Arnold had no way to get out of his mess, so he locked himself in his house and killed himself." She opened her eyes and looked at me. "Nothing is being said that we didn't already know or assume," she said.

"What about my Mom? Why is she trying to hurt me?" I shouted. I looked around my kitchen. France closed her eyes and listened.

"He's laughing. He says that it will only get

worse until you right the wrong." Her eyes flung open. "You have to right the wrong. It's a game to him. He's using this game to push you until you figure it out, to make you work harder." She looked worried.

"Do you know what he will do next?" I asked as I felt my heart begin to beat faster.

"I don't Tina, but this has to be figured out soon," she said and stood up. She didn't bring anything with her this time so she immediately went to the door.

"Keep me updated and come to me with anything that I can help you with," she said and left.

*****

My parents came home a few hours later. My father popped his head through the door. I just happened to be standing there because I heard their car door.

"Is she gone?" he said before coming in. I couldn't help but laugh at him.

"Yes, she's gone," I said through my giggles. He looked embarrassed and he opened the door all the way to let the rest of my family in.

"What did she say?" he asked. My mother stood beside him not saying anything but I could see that she was interested in what I had to say.

"She said that Mom was going to continue hurting me until I figure out how to right the wrong that Arnold has done," I said. I studied the expressions on both their faces. I could see that they both wanted to believe me but they couldn't bring themselves to. My mother put her head down and walked up the stairs. I helped my father get Tommy into his seat and I pulled some toys out for Heidi to play with. A few minutes later, my mother came back down and handed me a paper without looking at me.

"I dreamt that I needed to keep this from you and it was exactly where I had put it in my dream. I assume that it might be of some value to you," she said and walked by me and went straight to the kitchen.

I looked down at the paper that I held in my hand. It was the newspaper clipping that she said that she didn't have. This brought me hope. I smiled and made my way up to my room. I read and reread the article, but I didn't see anything that could help me. I felt my eyes get heavy, so I settled into my bed and under the covers for a nap. It didn't take long for sleep to engulf me.

I ran through the forest. It was dark and I was drenched in sweat. I lifted my arm to wipe my forehead. I ran as fast as my legs would go. I was filled with anger. I had so much rage running through my veins and it helped me to run that much faster. I looked at the trees as I ran by them. They were beautiful. The moon was reflecting off of them perfectly. But the rage that I felt had me concentrating on the path and my destination. *What is my destination?* I thought. I continued to run and I tried hard to think about why I was running and then I saw them. In the distance were two figures running. They were running for their lives; they were running from me! So much hate and rage filled me and I ran faster. I looked down at my right hand to make sure that I held my gun securely and in my left hand I held a shovel. I looked back up and kept my eyes on my targets. I was close, almost in arms reach; I threw the shovel. Amelia looked back at me, her eyes filled with terror. I smiled because I knew I had her. She tripped over a tree root that was protruding out of the ground and I made my move. I lunged forward and I had her by her arms. Holly basically gave herself to me while she fought me, trying to get her mother back.

I woke up drenched. I had to catch my breath, so I sat up and put my head in between my knees. When my breathing regulated, I looked up and Arnold was sitting at the end of my bed. I jumped at the sight of him.

"I was you?" I whispered. He nodded his head "yes."

"I was a killer?" I said more to myself than to him. He smirked. His smirk infuriated me.

"Well how do I right the wrong? I can't take back what you did!" I whispered loudly. He smiled his evil smile and then he disappeared.

"You can't just leave! Not now! Help me right your wrong!" I whispered loudly. But he didn't return. I could still feel the anger and rage that was flowing through my veins in my dream. I have never experienced so much hate.

I looked down at my hand; I was still clutching that article. I opened my hand and straightened it out and I reread it again and again until I grew bored of reading it. I pretty much memorized it.

I got off my bed and grabbed my phone and called Jack to tell him my new information.

*****

"Have you seen him since?" Emily asked when Jack and I updated her on all that's been happening when we went to her place for a visit.

"No, it's been two weeks since I found out that I am him and I have no idea on how I'm supposed to right the wrong," I said. "But at least he is giving me time I guess."

Emily and Jack nodded.

"Your hair is coming along nicely," Emily said and she touched my short strands. I ran my fingers through my five inches of hair. I had a headband in it with gel to help make it stand up into a spiked look. I never said it out loud, but I really liked my hair this way.

"Thanks, I'm really getting used to it. I may just cut it again when it grows back," I joked. "The college in Toronto has accepted my application. I start at the beginning of September," I announced. Jack gave me a huge bear hug and Emily gave me a quick sideways hug. Jack was staying in Cornwall but we promised each other that we'd spend every holiday together. It was only for two years with a three month break in the summer. I knew that we could pull it off. "I need to figure this out before I leave. I have less than two weeks before my Dad drives me up," I said. I pulled out the article for Emily to read.

"Do you see any clues in this?" I asked. She took the clipping and read it. Jack and I have read it over and over again and haven't noticed any clues. Maybe a new set of eyes could help.

"I don't know, Tina; maybe you'll have another dream?" she said and handed back the very worn out article to me.

"Maybe," I said and looked down. "I should get going. I told Heidi that I would have dinner at home every day until I leave." I smiled. "We have to get together though before I go," I said to Emily. She agreed and we hugged and said "goodbye."

*****

"Oh no, Tina!" Jack said when he turned onto my street. I looked up towards my house. There were two police cars parked in front of it.

"What's going on?" I said out loud. Jack pulled up in front of my driveway and we both ran out and into my house. I spotted my father right away.

"Dad! What's happening?" I asked him. He

turned around to look at me, but no words came out. I looked behind him and my mother was crying and screaming while she sat on the floor.

"What happened?" I screamed. I stared at her and demanded an answer.

"They are gone!" she screamed back at me through her sobs.

"Who is gone?" I asked and looked around. "Where are the kids?"

"They are gone, you idiot!" my mother screamed at me.

"The kids are gone? Well, where are they?" I asked.

"If I knew, would I be sitting here worrying about them?" she replied with attitude. I looked up at my father but he shrugged his shoulder. I turned around and went over to the officers.

"Where have you looked?" I asked. One officer turned to me. He was nice and had a welcoming smile.

"We searched the house so far. We will continue searching though and keep you updated," he said and turned back to the other officer.

I went back to my mother.

"What was your dream?" I asked. I stood in front of her with my arms crossed.

"Oh, so you're blaming me?" she accused.

"Yes, I am. Think about your dreams," I demanded. She glared at me. My father finally spoke up.

"I agree, dear, think about any dreams that

you may have had that included the kids in it," he said. I looked up at him and smiled. *Finally!* I thought.

"Don't you think I've been doing that, you lil' jerk?" she spat at me.

"What's your problem?" Jack asked her and he stepped in front of me. I gently moved him out of my way.

"It's fine, it's about time she talks to me," I said.

The police officers gathered up their reports and my father walked them to the door. It was the same conversation as the last time. "If you hear anything, call us and we'll do the same," they said and they walked out.

"You might as well leave, Jack. It's going to be a long night. I'm gonna go and check in the walls again and in the basement. So much for Arnold giving me time to figure things out," I said. He nodded and pursed his lips together.

"Okay, well keep me updated then," he said and kissed my forehead. I walked him to the door and thanked him again for everything.

I watched Jack leave then walked back to my mother.

"Where are they, Mom?" I shouted.

"Listen here!" she said. "If you hadn't brought in these evil spirits to begin with, we wouldn't be in this mess!" she screamed at me.

"Excuse me?" I shouted back as my mother got to her feet. "I told you everything before it got this bad. You chose to ignore me!" I screamed at her. Before I could bring my hand up, she slapped me on the cheek with the back of her hand. It knocked me back a couple of steps, but I stayed on my feet. My father stepped in between us and grabbed my mother by her shoulders.

"That is enough!" he yelled at her. "You've put her through enough!" He gently shoved her down on the couch. "Where are the kids, Janet?" he asked. He was glaring at her and he meant business. She looked away from him and stared at me.

"Why don't you ask her ghost? I have no idea where the kids are. Just this one," she said nodding towards me. I walked away. *Was Arnold making her say these things or is this how she felt?* I thought to myself. I heard my father tell my mother that he was going for a drive to look for the kids. I met him at the door.

"I don't think they are outside. I think she is hiding them, but she doesn't know it! We have to look in the house, just like before! We have to look in the walls and places that you've already looked!" I begged.

"I can't stay here. I don't feel like anything is getting accomplished. I will feel better once I take a drive around a couple of blocks just to see." He kissed me on my head. "I'll be back really soon. Stay out of your Mom's way until I get back," he warned.

"Okay, I will look in the house for them," I said and walked away. I decided to go upstairs and check my bedroom first since that's where Heidi was the first time. I looked everywhere: under my bed, under my desk, in corners, under my blankets. I opened my closet door and knocked on the wall that my father had fixed after tearing it down.

"Heidi! Are you in there?" I shouted with my face pressed against the wall. I listened but heard nothing. I tried everyone's rooms and closets; I banged on all of the walls yelling Heidi's name. I didn't yell for Tommy since he was too little to know any better. I decided to try my luck downstairs in the basement. I ran down the stairs taking two steps at a time and I did the same with the basement stairs. Once I got to the basement, I immediately started yelling for Heidi. I looked under boxes and planks of wood.

"Heidi! Where are you?" I screamed. I found an old trunk that we stored our winter coats in. I walked slowly towards it and opened it quickly. I dug my hands in and started pulling everything out, but they weren't there either. I heard footsteps behind me.

"Heidi, sweetie, is that you?" I shouted and turned to follow the sound. As I passed by some stacked boxes, my mother jumped out from behind them and tackled me to the floor. I screamed, but she was determined. She shoved, what I assumed was a sock, in my mouth and managed to pin me on my stomach. She tied my hands behind my back and my feet together with an old skipping rope and stood me up. She literally dragged me up the stairs and out the side door. She struggled, but she managed to get her rear car door open and threw me in. Just as I thought she was through and was going to close the door, she buckled the seat belt in behind me and tied my skipping rope to it. She did the same with my feet on the other side. She closed the door and rushed around to the driver's seat.

She peeled out of the driveway and we were gone. I hoped in my heart that she was taking me to my sister and brother. Maybe I'd have a chance to save them. I struggled in the back seat of my mother's sedan. I pulled and tugged but the seat belt was locked in place. I tried to slide my hands down to the buckle but she must have attached the rope to the corner so it wasn't giving me any slack. I eventually gave in, lied there and waited for her to stop the car. After about ten or fifteen minutes of driving, she pulled over to the side of the road. I heard the gravel underneath the tires. She got out of the car. I heard her open up the trunk and struggle to take something out, and then slam it closed again. She opened the rear door and unbuckled the seat belts and pulled me out. I tried kicking her, but she seemed unusually strong. Without any warning, she threw me onto Heidi's wagon and tied another skipping rope around me and the wagon. I was still struggling but it was useless. She was stronger than I was. She securely tied the rope and looked up at the trees. I did the same and then I let my eyes wander around to scope out my surroundings. We were at the forest!

The one where Amelia and Holly were buried.

My mother went to the back of the car and grabbed a shovel. She took the handle of the wagon and started to pull the wagon with me in it through the very dark trail. I twisted and turned trying to make myself fall out but she had tied the ropes tight. I tried screaming and struggling but I couldn't move. I watched all the familiar trees go by as we passed them. I couldn't stop trembling and the butterflies were ramming the walls of my stomach trying hard to get out. My mouth became dry and I started gagging on the sock that was shoved deep in my mouth. I tried using my tongue to dislodge it, but it wouldn't budge. I breathed deeply through my nose and waited for her to stop.

Finally, after what felt like hours of walking, she stopped. I looked around and spotted the tree that Amelia and Holly were buried near. We were right under it. She walked away from me and started to dig up the graves. She dug for a long time while I did everything I could to escape. I looked around for my sister and brother, but there was no sign of them. I tried to pull my wrists out of the rope, but it was too tight. I waited, but I didn't stop struggling to free myself. I looked over when I heard my mother throw the shovel. She was coming for me. She grabbed me by my shoulders, pulled me out of the wagon and dragged me over to the hole she had dug. I hoped that the bodies were not exposed. I didn't have time to look before my mother shoved me and I fell into the hole hitting the side with my head on the way down. I screamed muffled screams; none of the sounds were loud enough for anyone to hear. I was panicking, doing what I could to untie the rope from my feet first. I was able to reach it but with my shaking and panicking and the soil my mother was throwing on me, my fingers refused to work properly. I tried to take deep breaths, but each time I did I inhaled dirt up my nose leaving me to choke silently on it.

My body was starting to get covered with the dirt when finally I was able to bring my hands under my bottom and around to my front. I pulled the sock out of my mouth and threw it. I took a few deep breaths and then I started to scream. I screamed with only a second in between each breath. My mother didn't stop. She didn't even flinch; she just continued to throw the dirt on my head. I stopped screaming and started gnawing at the skipping rope that was around my wrists, but I would throw in a few screams in between. I knew that nobody lived close enough to hear me, but my survival instincts didn't let me stop.

I heard someone! I stopped screaming and moving for a second. My mother did too because the soil stopped falling on me.

"Tina!" I heard my father yell. I screamed louder than I thought I was capable of. "Tina! I'm coming!" my father screamed. My mother hurriedly continued to throw the soil on me. She was going much quicker than before, but my father came up behind her. I didn't see anything, but I heard him fall to the ground after the shovel hit him.

"Dad!" I screamed. "Dad! Wake up!" The ground was coming up around me making it hard to keep my head above it. I threw my head back to keep the dirt out of my mouth and screamed until I was covered into the ground. I couldn't breathe anymore. I dug a hole above my head to let in any air but it was no longer working. I thought about Heidi and sweet, sweet Tommy. I thought about Jack and Emily and I thought about my parents. My mother loved me so much at one time. We were best friends and now she's buried me alive. I felt myself go unconscious, and I didn't feel anything after that.

Chapter 12

I woke up in the hospital with my father hovering above me.

"How did you save me, Dad?" I asked him. He smiled at me. "I'm your Dad, I have super powers, don't I?" he asked me. I looked at his face; his left side was bruised and swollen.

"Of course you do, you always did," I replied. And I hugged him.

"How long have I been here?" I asked.

"Not long, sweetheart, just a couple of hours. I had time to carry you to my car and drive you here. They hooked you up to a couple of machines and you woke up," he told me.

"Where is Mom?" I asked with a note of worry. "She wasn't herself. Is she okay?"

"Yes, she is at home worried sick about you. She claims that she doesn't remember anything," he told me.

"How did you know where we were?" I asked.

"I wasn't gone far when I took my drive to look for the kids and I saw your mother's car drive by, so I followed her," he explained.

"Okay, so what took you so long to get to us?" I asked. He shook his head.

"My tire blew. I spun out into the road and

there were pieces of my tire everywhere; it was strange. I changed it as fast as I could and drove around looking for your mother's car. When I found it, it was beside a trail. I walked through the forest assuming that's where she was. I hoped that she was leading me to Heidi and Tommy, but then I heard your screams," he told me.

"And Heidi and Tommy? Please don't tell me she buried them too!" I asked and I couldn't stop the tears that flowed down my cheeks and onto my blanket. He hugged me.

"They are fine! She took them to your Aunt Nora and Uncle Mike's. She claims to not remember doing that either," he told me.

"Oh good! I was so worried about them!" I told him.

"The doctor said that once you wake up, if all is good with your vital signs, you could leave in an hour. I'm going to go and tell them that you've woken up," he said with a smile. He left the room and within seconds, Jack came in.

"I shouldn't have left! I knew something was wrong with your Mom. I should have stayed!" he said and took my hand.

"I'm fine, Jack. Don't worry. I'm leaving in an hour." I smiled.

"You're not fine! You're in the hospital. Again," he said.

Just then my father came back with a doctor; Jack backed away. My father nodded his head at Jack and Jack did the same.

"How are you doing Tina?" the doctor asked. I read his tag: Dr. Johnson.

"I feel fine," I told him.

"Your Dad tells me that you were playing around in the forest and fell in a pre-dug hole. What were you doing in the forest?" he asked. I looked quickly at my father but all he did was raise his eyebrows.

"I wanted to try smoking so I walked into the forest to not get caught," I lied. Dr. Johnson laughed.

"Well, I hope you've learned a lesson here. Smoking is not good for you." He continued to laugh at his own joke as he checked my vitals. I looked over at my father who tried hard to hide his smile, which made Jack and I smile too. We all burst out laughing together and the doctor joined us.

"Well, everything looks good. You are free to leave in one hour," he looked at his watch. "Ten o'clock seems about right. And remember, no smoking!" he said as he laughed his way out of my room.

I shook my head at the doctor's bad joke. Jack and my father both waited with me. At ten o'clock, a nurse came in to check my vitals once more and told me that I was free to go. My father drove me home and Jack followed close behind us in his car.

"He's going to miss you when you go off to college," my father said as he stared at Jack through his rear view mirror.

"I'll miss him too, but we'll see each other on holidays and there's the internet and phone calls. It will be like I never left," I said smiling. "Besides, it's only for two years."

"He's a good kid," my father said and looked away from the rear view, concentrating on the road ahead of us.

When we arrived at home, my father stayed in his car.

"I'm going to go and pick up Heidi and Tommy. Jack will stay here with you until I get back," my father said and backed out of the driveway. When he got on the road, he rolled down his window and pointed to Jack. He warned, "Don't let her out of your sight."

Jack wrapped his arm around my shoulder. "Not a chance," he said as my father drove off.

"Let's sit outside until he gets back, Jack," I said.

We sat on the front porch and didn't say much. He let me put my head on his shoulder and we waited for my siblings to return.

"Tina!" Heidi yelled when she jumped out of the car.

"Hey, my girl!" I yelled back and ran down the steps to pick her up.

"Where did you go?" I asked as I held her.

"I played with Aunt Nora," she said and laughed as she hugged me tight around my neck.

"Hey, lil' man!" I said as my father approached with Tommy. It felt so good to see them both safe.

Jack gave them each a squeeze and left for the night. I had a feeling that he'd be back bright and early the next day, since he had no trust in my mother until things were sorted out.

*****

"I'm fine! It's been days!" I said to Jack when he told me that he wasn't taking me back to the forest. I begged. "I need to go back! I have one week left to fix this. That's not a lot of time! You'll be with me the whole time!"

"Fine," he said.

We were sitting on my front porch. We've been doing this from morning until night since the incident.

"Good. Grab two shovels and throw them in the trunk," I ordered.

He did what I wanted and we left.

"So, what's your plan?" he asked me while we were on our way to the graves.

"I want to dig up their graves to see if they are really there," I said.

"And if they are?" he asked.

"I'm not sure, but we'll deal with it then," I said.

We walked through the familiar grounds of the forest. We turned off the trail, where the root

242

stuck out of the ground, and walked over to the beautiful tree. We stood under it for a second and the image of me buried under the dug up soil gave me chills. I shrugged it off.

"I guess we just dig," I said and shoved my shovel into the ground.

We dug for a while without saying anything. I removed my sweater and continued. "We should have brought water," I said. My mouth was dry.

"You said shovels. You didn't mention anything about water," he joked.

Jack dug his shovel into the ground and we heard a crunch. He stopped and looked at me. I dropped down to my knees and used my hands to move the dirt. I knew why we were here and I knew what we were looking for but, when I saw the bone sticking out of the ground, I couldn't help but jump up and scream. I screamed like it was someone I knew for years that was buried in this grave. I felt like I knew Amelia and Holly. I stopped screaming and sobbed into Jack's arms. We climbed out of the grave together and went back to the car where I had left my cell phone. I called 911 and told them that we had found two bodies buried in the forest. I hung up and looked at Jack.

"Giving them a proper burial. That is a good way to right someone's wrong, don't you think?" I asked Jack. He nodded his head and we waited for the police together.

When the police arrived, we brought them over to the graves. I pulled out the article, which I had stuffed in my pocket, and gave it to one of the police officers. I said, "I am certain that the bodies in the ground belong to Amelia and Holly Trepherd. They deserve a proper burial."

He took the newspaper clipping from me and asked how I knew where to find them. I looked at him straight in the eyes and asked, "Do you believe in ghosts?"

He smiled and took down my name, address and phone number and told me that they would contact me with any questions. Jack and I turned and followed the trail out of the forest. We didn't look back.

*****

I did have an officer come to my house. He asked me a few question on how I knew the whereabouts of the graves and how I knew that it was Amelia and Holly. I told him the truth to an extent, but just the basics. He didn't laugh at me. He told me that we had done a great job on investigating and solving an old case.

Now, I stood in front of the long mirror in my room and stared at the reflection of a girl on her way to college. My hair wasn't boring anymore, it was funky. I loved messing it up with hair gel, making it stand up in soft spikes, and adding a headband as an accessory. I wore a blue V-neck shirt that went down to my hips, a black pair of leggings and knee high black boots. I felt good and pretty. My mother came to my door with a smile. She was beautiful and back to her old self.

"You look wonderful, dear! College material for sure!" she said.

She came to me and we hugged. We had been able to go shopping together earlier for all of my school supplies. It gave us a chance to catch up and talk. It was nice. It was also very peaceful now in my house. There were no more dark corners or eerie feelings.

"Jack and Emily are both downstairs waiting to say "goodbye," dear. Are you ready?" she asked me.

"Yes, I just need my bag and I'm good to go," I said as I went to get my bag.

"Oh no, dear, let me get it for you," she said and picked up my bag as we headed downstairs together.

There were a lot of tears along with our goodbyes.

"I'm coming back you guys!" I said through my own tears. I broke free from the people who loved me as much as I loved them and got into the car with my father. I looked at my side mirror as we drove away and watched Heidi wave goodbye until I couldn't see them anymore.

Epilogue

I came home for Thanksgiving and everyone was waiting for me. Jack was there with his warm embrace and soft kisses. Emily was there with her witty comments and funny self. We all had a wonderful Thanksgiving together.

"Did they bury Amelia and Holly?" I asked Jack when we were alone.

"They did," he said with his brilliant smile. "Do you want to visit them?" he asked already getting ready to stand up.

I laughed and said, "Of course I do."

We both got up and went to his car. The graveyard was about twenty minutes away, so we had a chance to talk about my new school and his new job. I held his hand as he drove and I stared at him a lot. I missed him so much.

When we arrived, he pulled up right beside their graves. I stepped out of the car.

"Do you want me to come with you?" he asked.

"No, I'm fine," I said and walked over to their graves.

I was pleasantly surprised to see that they had tombstones. Nothing out of the ordinary was written on them, but at least they had their own stones and a proper burial. I talked to them for a few minutes and then stood up and walked back towards the car. I looked back at their stones and jumped at the sight of Arnold standing in between the stones. He was looking down at them. I stared at him without moving a muscle until he glanced up at me. He smiled a handsome smile and nodded his head at me before he disappeared. A feeling of greatness washed over me. I'd accomplished something big: the Trepherd family can now rest in peace.

Copyhouse Press

CPSIA information can be obtained at www.ICGtesting.com
Printed in the USA
LVOW07s1657191015

458864LV00034B/1861/P